FIVE YEARS ON A ROCK

Genealogy

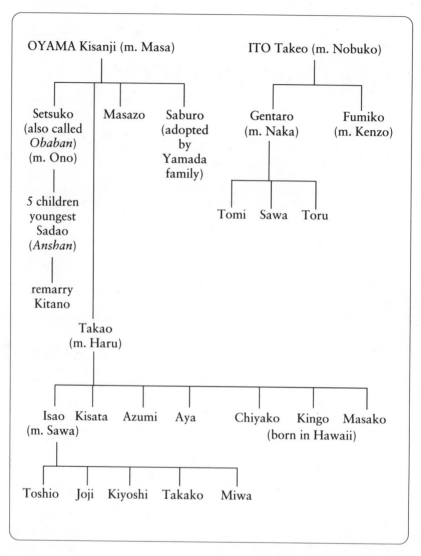

Notes:

Haru (Takao Oyama's wife) and Naka (Gentaro Ito's wife) are first cousins.

Tokiko (Toki-chan) is Naka's sister.

The suffix "*chan*" is a term of endearment (e.g., "Set-chan" for Setsuko).

"*Anshan*" is a corruption of "*ani-san*" (elder brother).

FIVE * YEARS
ON * A * ROCK

Milton Murayama

 UNIVERSITY OF HAWAII PRESS • HONOLULU

Milton Murayama
12/17/94

FOR THE FAMILY

Library of Congress Cataloging-in-Publication Data
Murayama, Milton.
Five years on a rock / Milton Murayama.
    p. cm.
ISBN 0–8248–1647–1 (acid-free paper)
PS3563.U723F58 1994
813'.54—dc20   94–9806
                                                        CIP

A version of the first chapter of this work was published in the *Seattle Review,*
Spring/Summer 1988.

University of Hawaii Press books are printed on acid-free paper and meet the
guidelines for permanence and durability of the Council on Library Resources

Designed by Kenneth Miyamoto

PART I ✳ *1914–1915*

1 · The Proposal

Aunt Toki-chan said it first: "Sawa-chan is like a face painted on an egg. She's for Koso."

"Sawa-chan is so cute, she's for Koso," the others echoed. The teasing stopped about the time I entered first grade, but I assumed the match had been sealed. I was to be Koso-san's wife.

In 1872 the new government replaced the old rice tax with a 3 percent tax on the value of the land, payable only in cash. So after a couple of bad harvests, the farmers lost their land to the money-lenders and big landholders. But it wasn't the land tax that ruined our family.

Grandfather had two children, Father and Aunt Fumiko. He was so fond of Aunt Fumiko he decided to adopt a husband for her so that he could keep her at home. It was unheard of. Only a family without a son adopts a husband. The adopted husband gives up his name (some say his manhood) and adopts his wife's name. He inherits the family property and continues the family line. Many adopted husbands think they're acquiring instant wealth, but most are treated like servants by their wives and mothers-in-law. The proverb says, "If you have a handful of bran, don't become an adopted husband." Childless families adopt their nephews or grandsons, but one never heard of an unrelated husband being adopted into a poor family.

Kenzo Ishida, now Kenzo Ito, came to live with us, and immediately our home shook with shouts and curses. Grandfather and Kenzo-san nearly came to blows. I'd never seen Grandfather with such bulging eyes. Even I could see Kenzo-san was a crook. His posture was crooked. He was furious when he learned he was inheriting only half of our five-acre farm. He sold his share of the farm, then stole Grandfather's seal and sold another acre. When Aunt Fumiko finally divorced him, there were only one and one-half acres left of our once-large farm.

Grandfather died soon afterward. I was seven then. The war with Russia had just ended. We went to Togo Station, waving our little flags to welcome home the victorious soldiers. But the celebration was short. The wounded, dressed in white kimonos, were everywhere. So many boys in the neighboring villages had been killed. Our island of Kyushu prided itself on its great warriors. We'd fought off the Mongols twice—we were the core of the modern army—but now the government didn't even have money to rehabilitate the crippled or help families left without their men. The farmers kept losing their land, and the young men unable to find work were returning to the overcrowded farms now owned by the big landowners and moneylenders. The new owners leased the land to the former owners for 60 percent of the crops. The samurai rulers had said during feudal times, "See that the peasant has just enough to live on and no more." It was still the same in the new, supposedly classless society.

It was a sad funeral. Our home, our trees, our yard, even our clothes looked shabby. The Shibatas—Aunt Toki-chan and her family—looked brisk and energetic by comparison. Koso-san was so tall for an eleven year old. I felt so awed I couldn't raise my eyes to look at him.

"Poor Father," Mother said. "*Hako iri musume ni mushi ga tsuita.* A worm has gotten to the daughter-in-the-box."

"You can't trust an outsider," Aunt Toki-chan said.

Father leased the remaining one and one-half acres and went to work as a clerk at the county office in Togo. He played the stock market and kept losing.

"I'm only trying to recover what Father lost," he would say.

"But you know nothing about stocks!" Mother would reply.

"It's all luck!"

"It's not all luck! It's hard work. You always take the lazy way!"

"Shut up!" He would walk out.

"There is no easy way."

After three years only half an acre remained.

In 1910 the government made eighth-grade education compulsory. "You'll have two more years of vacation," Mother said. The next year Father sold the remaining one-quarter acre to provide a dowry for Tomi. There were only three of us: older sister Tomi, myself, and little brother Toru.

"We'd have enough for Sawa's dowry too if you hadn't gambled it away," Mother said.

We'll raise the dowry somehow, I thought. The Shibatas acquired more and more land. They built a large new house, which Koso would inherit some day. He was now a tall, handsome five feet seven inches. He had been drafted and was stationed at an artillery battery in Shimonoseki.

Several months after the outbreak of the Great War, Father got a letter from Mr. Taniguchi, Mother's first cousin. Japan was allied with Great Britain and had declared war on Germany, but no troops were sent to Europe.

"He asks if we'll be home the day after New Year's," Father said.

"I wonder what he wants?" Mother asked.

Money, I thought. Creditors were always coming to our home, and Mr. Taniguchi had inherited his late father's pawnshop.

Mr. Taniguchi arrived midmorning dressed in his formal *hakama* skirt. He had Mother's wide cheekbones and button nose. His clothes were crisp, his *tabi* socks immaculate, but he slouched badly.

We served the New Year's dish of *ozoni.* Mr. Taniguchi picked at the food and talked about the weather, the war, inflation, taxes, foreclosures, everything except what he'd come for.

I'd stepped down into the kitchen and was heating more *sake,* wondering if Koso-san was home for New Year's. What did Mr. Taniguchi want? What was so urgent? We didn't owe him money. He lived in Kokura. His mother and my mother's father were siblings in the Yoshida family.

"Sawa, Sawa," Father called.

"Hai." I hurried out and kneeled on the tatami and bowed.

"The Oyama family in Hawaii has asked for your hand . . . for their number one son," he said.

"Eh!" I gasp and try to pull in my jerky, twitchy body. My head flops on the tatami; my neck is jelly.

"How do you feel?" Father's voice is far off.

"Eh!"

"What do you say?"

"I'll do whatever you wish!" a high-pitched voice squeaks above my head.

"She probably needs time to think about it," Mother says.

"Excuse me." I skirt backward, head bowed. I slide open the shoji behind me, bow deeply, back out, and close the shoji.

I nearly bump into a tipsy Mr. Kawahara, our neighbor. *"Gomen nasai. Akemashite omedetoh . . ."*

I bow and stumble. My eyes roll back—I can't faint now! The blackness passes and there's a rush of fragments, white on coach green, a single persimmon on bare branches, a blur of pink. Suddenly I'm seeing things for the first time! I shake my head, but nothing comes back. *This is silly,* I think to myself. This is the bamboo thicket in the corner that belonged to the whole village. I used to come here to cut bamboo shoots. I can even point out the cuts I made. So why do they look so strange?

"Uncle Asthma will get angry," I remember Mother saying every time I did something that might trigger an asthma attack. Inhaling was no problem, but the air built up inside till you felt like exploding. I'm exhaling easily now, mouth wide open. The moment passes. The tall green bamboo stems look friendly again.

I walk the dirt road to the torii gate. The giant cryptomeria stands beside it. At the top of the many steps is the shrine. I pull the twisted rope to the rusty bell, press my hands together, bow, and pray, "Please, San-O-sama, save me." I pray over and over, making sure San-O-sama hears me.

Suddenly I'm shivering. The light is luminous, a glow of winter gray under an overcast sky. Scrub oaks dot the rolling hills. The dry paddies in the valley look like postage stamps. The village is a cluster of thatched roofs. San-O-sama is the guardian deity of the village of Ikeura. We celebrated the planting and harvest at the shrine. We cleaned the spacious hall, hung up new paintings done by the villagers, and offered food at the altar. The wooden building had burned down once, and the whole village pitched in and rebuilt it. The farms around Ikeura were on high ground, and the villagers had built a dam and shared the water. We were family.

The steps are so steep, the treads so narrow, it's always harder walking down. Am I the only one who believed all the baby talk? What about Koso-san? He hadn't given me any sign that he was even aware of me. What if I waited and he married somebody else? Everybody would say, "She's the abalone who fell in love with its rock." But why should he marry me? He could have his choice of beautiful *rich* girls.

"Where have you been? You'll catch a cold. I sent Toru with your *haori,"* Mother said.

"Mr. Taniguchi wants an answer in a month," Father said.

"You don't have to go if you don't want to," Mother said.

What about Koso-san? Have you spoken to your older sister? When we were babies, she said I was for Koso-san.... I would phrase and rephrase the question and approach Mother, but I'd lose my courage and say, "Father wants me to go, doesn't he?"

"You don't have to go if you don't want to."

"What do you think?"

"It's what you think that matters."

I walked to my sewing class in a trance. I'd been living in a fantasy. But I'd never dreamed I'd be leaving my ancestral home. Picture brides for Hawaii and America were always from other villages.

"Don't blame everything on your father." Mother and Father were at it again, unaware I had sneaked into the earthen entryway. I kicked off my slippers and crept into the kitchen.

"It was his fault! The five acres were my inheritance!"

"It's bad enough not having any ambition. You have an addiction like an alcoholic. Instead of *sake,* it's gambling. Now you want to push Sawa to become a picture bride. Just for the engagement gift."

"Shut up!" He slid open the shoji and stepped into his clogs.

I made myself small as he glanced into the kitchen.

"It hurts, but we have to talk about it," Mother yelled after him.

A couple of days later, I went to see Yoshida Jukichi-san, who was Mother's uncle and headman of the village. He presided at the councils of our extended family.

"The Oyamas are like your family. They've lost their farm," he said. "Brides leaving for Hawaii don't need dowries. In addition, engagement gifts from Hawaii are in cash, and they're ten times larger than those in Japan. I've been told some are as high as 2,000 yen [$1,000]. So leaving for Hawaii means you'll be saving your parents $400 in dowry, besides getting them, let's say, given the Oyamas' finances, a $500 engagement gift."

"You think I should go?"

"That's up to you." He kept sticking out his tongue and scraping it back against his teeth.

"It'd be the filial thing to do, wouldn't it?"

"It would be good for the family."

My sewing teacher, Mrs. Taketa, lived in the next village four kilometers away. I loved the walk. It was the only time I could be alone to think. *Since I'm a woman and can't amount to anything,* I thought, *I might as well go to Hawaii.*

"I've made up my mind," I said that evening when we were preparing supper.

"Are you sure?"

"Yes."

"You shouldn't let our fighting influence you."

"I talked to Uncle Jukichi."

Father was in a good mood at supper. "It'd be better if Sawa married the second son. The number one son has a reputation of being undisciplined."

If the Oyamas were so hard pressed, they probably couldn't afford $500, or even $400. But even $350 would buy back one *tan*. It'd be my gift, one-quarter acre producing five bushels of rice per year. In the old days the one-quarter acre produced enough to feed an adult for a year.

"What is Mrs. Oyama like?" I asked Mother.

"I don't know."

"But you're first cousins."

"That doesn't mean a thing. You're a stranger unless you belong to the same extended family."

"She must be very strict."

"Hmmm. Maybe. She used to run her father's pawnshop."

Mr. Taniguchi returned in early March for the exchange of engagement gifts. Father gave the traditional *hakama* skirt and received a pair of folding fans and money in an envelope. Father looked irritated, almost angry, after Mr. Taniguchi left. Throughout the afternoon and evening people kept calling. *Must be creditors,* I thought.

We're taught from childhood not to be nosy, but I simply had to ask. After all, it was a gift in my name.

I waited till we were alone in the kitchen that night and stammered, "How much? . . . I mean the *yuino* . . ."

"Three hundred fifty dollars, but it's all been taken away," Mother said matter-of-factly.

"It was supposed to be my gift to you and Father."

"Shikata ga nai."

It can't be helped. The farmers said it when typhoons or droughts destroyed their crops, when they couldn't get a decent price for their rice, when they lost their farms. It can't be helped; it's fate.

2 · Marriage by Proxy

The wedding was set for April. Mrs. Sueoka from the neighboring village came to put up my hair. I wore my powder-blue kimono Mother had bought in Hakata, and we walked the five kilometers to the county office in Togo. Mr. Taniguchi met us in a black suit and vest and acted as his nephew's proxy. He gave me a photo of Isao-san and I gave him one of myself. Then the official wrote down our birth dates and addresses on the application form. He recorded my height, four feet ten inches, my weight, ninety-five pounds, and examined my fingertips. "They're all whorls except the left thumb, which is loops," he said, writing. Then he married us.

The government had agreed in 1907 not to issue any more passports to laborers seeking work in America. But those already there could send for their wives and children. Those married by proxy qualified as wives and were called "picture brides."

I studied my husband's photo. The eyes, nose, and mouth were so well shaped and symmetrical. How tall was he? I tried to remember the one time I'd seen him. I was about five. He and his brothers had come to our home to pick persimmons. He must've been nine then, so his parents were already in Hawaii, and he was living with his grandparents. The three boys had looked like ragamuffins.

A few weeks later I got a letter from my husband. "Don't bring any fancy kimonos. The style of life is so different here. It's so hot, a futon is useless. Just bring what you can carry. You can buy the appropriate tropical clothes in Hawaii. We await your safe arrival."

"He's got a beautiful hand," Mother said.

"Good calligraphy is character," Father said. "Look how straight and upright his writing is."

A week later I returned from my sewing lesson and announced, *"Tada-ima!"* As I stepped into the entryway I was startled by excited voices beyond the shoji. *They're fighting again,* I thought. But it wasn't Father's voice. Then I noticed a pair of brand-new slippers on the steps.

"I'm telling you again! It's too late!" Mother's voice came from beyond the shoji.

"Why were you in such a hurry?" a man's voice demanded.

"Why were you so slow?!"

"We had to call a council. Then we had to go to Shimonoseki to ask Koso. He said yes, he wants to marry Sawa. He said he had taken it for granted." It was Koso's father!

"Why didn't you tell us you were deliberating? We're only twelve kilometers away! When she dawdled, naturally we thought she wasn't interested."

"But why did you rush it so? Others take six months to decide such things!"

"You have to be married for six months before they give you a passport! It's just like older sister. She's avoided us ever since we lost our farm. Naturally we thought she didn't want anything to do with a ruined family. Now she plays the injured party. She can't have it both ways," Mother said.

"I don't believe she's already married."

"Go check the Oyama register."

"I will."

I put the sewing basket on the kitchen floor and wandered in the warm spring air. The paddies were underwater. Plums in pink bonnets. I took the short way through the paddies to the giant cryptomeria and torii gate. I remembered the panic barely three months ago. Now I felt only sadness. Even if I climbed the steps, what could I ask? Please, San-O-sama, turn back the clock? Even Koso's father would give up once he saw my name in the Oyama family register. But why hadn't Koso said something? Why was everybody so polite and reserved? Why were we so quiet? We're taught from childhood to be meek and well mannered. But this time our future was at stake! So why didn't I shout, "What about Koso? What about *me?!*"

After supper that night, we stood in the kitchen preparing the next day's breakfast.

"Mr. Shibata was here today," Mother said, washing the rice.

"Oh." I was peeling taro roots for miso soup. When cooked for a long time, these roots crumbled in your mouth, saturated with the taste of miso.

"It's probably better this way. Older sister's nose has grown so tall. She'd treat you like a poor cousin if you married Koso. She's changed so much since she's gotten so rich . . ."

Her voice barely reached me. I loved the earthy feel of these little roots. Their skins were tough and their meat slimy, but they weren't supposed to make your eyes water.

". . . the Oyamas are more our match. We're both bankrupt families. Father, by the way, was so pleased when the proposal came from Hawaii. He didn't know how he was going to raise the money for your dowry."

I washed my hands and wiped my eyes and blew my nose.

"I've made up my mind," I said. "I'm throwing off Koso-san and embracing Isao-san and Hawaii."

3 · Departure

"I would like to sew the womenfolk kimonos stenciled with the Oyama crest," I wrote my husband.

"Sew one for yourself, too. We've written Uncle Taniguchi to accompany you," he wrote back.

I walked the ten kilometers to Omaru village to get a sample of the family crest. Grandmother Oyama hadn't expected me, and she looked haggard. "I have to baby-sit three grandchildren," she sighed. She had a shapely oval face and delicate white skin.

"*Sumimasen,*" I apologized to Uncle Taniguchi when he came for me.

Hakata is the older half of Fukuoka City. Small fabric shops lined the alleys, and bolts of silk were pushed into cubicles against the wall. The shopkeeper would bring down one bolt, then another. "Let's see how that one looks against this," I'd say, or, "That other one." By mid-afternoon Uncle Taniguchi looked exhausted. He slouched more. "I'm sorry," I said each time we left a shop.

But anyone can learn to sew kimonos. All it takes is the patience to do the laborious hand stitching. The cloth is cut and stitched in straight lines. A single basic pattern fits all sizes, and the wearer and the obi give it shape. The beauty is in the simple, free-falling straight lines. Even the colors are matched by tradition—plum blossom for winter or white outside/red inside, wisteria for spring or lavender with blue lining. But I wanted to do something unique, to match colors you'd think would clash. The traditional is too predictable.

I kept examining cloth after cloth, singly, in pairs, in threes. You can match clashing colors only if they have complementing patterns imbedded in the color, but there are no fixed rules. "How much is this?" I asked each time. The fabrics with patterns were so expensive, I didn't even bother to ask Uncle Taniguchi. Besides, I would need solid colors if the family crests were to be stenciled in white. I would cut corners on the linings and stitch them to upper halves of cotton.

Uncle Taniguchi sighed as he counted out the money. *He must think I'm a spendthrift*, I thought.

We ate pork cutlets at a little restaurant, then spent the night at Tenrikyo Church. The next morning we went back to the shop to pick up the fabric, two pieces of which the shopkeeper had stenciled with the Oyama crest—three paulownia leaves in a circle.

"I can go back by myself," I said when we got to the Hakata Station.

"Are you sure?"

"I'm fine," I insisted.

He agreed reluctantly.

✳ ✳ ✳

"These will be your graduation pieces," Mrs. Taketa said. I did Chiyako's flower print first. Next I worked on my own navy blue with white lining. Then Aunt Kitano's brown with chartreuse, and finally Mother-in-law Haru's charcoal with blood red. Mrs. Taketa said over and over that you reinforce all the Japanese values in kimono sewing. All the homonyms were there. "Basting," or *shitsuke,* could also be written with the characters for "disciplining." *Eri o awaseru*—"to match the collars"—could mean also *eri wo tadasu*—"to straighten oneself." Posture was all-important. *Orime tadashisa*—"straightness of the folds"—meant also "correctness of manners." I had to be attentive to the smallest detail. I blotted out everything else when I sewed.

"Now you can sew for money," Mrs. Taketa said.

✳ ✳ ✳

The waiting was forever. Suddenly the passport arrived. Uncle Taniguchi got me a berth on the *Tenyo Maru,* which was leaving for Hawaii in ten days. My heart fluttered and fluttered; food sat in a lump in my stomach. I packed and repacked the kimonos in the wicker basket, folding them on their vertical lines. The lines had to be straight. A kimono could be unraveled and resewn any number of times without marring the beauty of its straight lines.

I went back to our deity's shrine. "Please, San-O-sama, I would like to borrow a handful of Ikeura soil to take with me to Hawaii." I put a handful of loose dirt into a cotton pouch I had sewn. "I will bring it back without fail in five years."

The women of the village brought their homegrown vegetables and chickens and worked all day preparing *nishime,* sushi, and red rice. The fishmonger in Togo delivered the fish for sashimi, a sea bream to be cooked whole for good luck, sea urchins, lobsters, and fish cakes. The brewer brought two five-gallon tubs of *sake.* "It's the war," they said when Mother complained about the prices. She had saved enough of the $350 to pay for the fish and *sake.*

Koso and his parents didn't come, but Grandmother Oyama had come the day before. She looked like a new person in her black kimono with its pattern of cranes. Her hair was neatly combed.

"Let's bathe together," she said.

We scrubbed each other's backs, then sat knee-to-knee in the steaming tub. She looked beautiful for her age.

"You know," she said, "Takao said he was returning in five years. That was thirteen years ago. It's his duty as number one son to look after his parents, but he's left everything to Masazo, who didn't inherit a cent. Not only that, Takao leaves his two youngest children with me when I'm already looking after Setsuko's boy. It's a thankless job. That's what happens when your master dies young."

"There must be a reason," I mumbled.

"What?"

"That he can't return in five years."

"He claims it's because his wife is sick all the time."

"What's wrong with her?"

"I don't know. He claims she needs a private doctor. The plantation doctors can't find anything wrong. It's too bad Saburo wasn't the number one son. We gave him away as an adopted husband. He was studying in Germany before the war. He's in England now. He was the smartest of the boys. It was so hard to say no. The Yamadas promised to send him to Europe to study."

"It's nice to hear of someone succeeding as an adopted husband. They say most of them are miserable."

"It must've been difficult for him to marry the oldest of the daughters. Your husband, by the way, went to live with them to at-

14

tend middle school. Back in 1908, 1909. He ran away after a year. I guess it must've irked Saburo's wife to find a vestige of an Oyama in the house."

"Have you met her?"

"She's so ugly they couldn't have married her off to anybody but an adopted husband."

"Well, but he's succeeding; that's the important thing."

"As a Yamada, not an Oyama. He'll probably become the first doctor of chemistry in Japan."

She looked so composed. There was no bitterness in her voice. The story was that she had been a maid at the Oyamas, and the late Grandfather Oyama, who was engaged to somebody else, got her pregnant. Her ex-boyfriend set fire to the Oyama house. Grandfather Oyama sued the ex-boyfriend. But her parents said they didn't want their daughter marrying somebody who was so despicable as to invite arson. So Grandfather Oyama dropped the suit and married the maid, who gave birth to Aunt Setsuko, now Mrs. Kitano. Father-in-law Takao was the second child.

The party began soon after dark. Mrs. Sueoka came early and did my hair. I used to get stage fright even when I spoke in class. Now everybody was fussing over me.

I sat at the head of the table. Father gave a short speech, then Uncle Taniguchi, then Uncle Yoshida. Then they all turned to me. I bowed and shouted, "Thank you for all the kindness you have shown me and my family! I shall never forget my happy memories of Ikeura!"

The men and women sat on the straw mats on both sides of the table and ate and toasted, "We're losing the prettiest girl in Ikeura"; "We're losing the flower of Ikeura." The men's faces got redder and puffier as the night wore on. They pitched and jerked and shouted. Only Grandmother Oyama stayed in focus, a beautiful oval face with a widow's peak. She proposed the last toast. "Sawa-chan is the flower of filial piety, but she needs her rest."

I hardly slept, combing my mind for anything I might have forgotten. The three kimonos folded in their vertical lines, the sewing kit in the smaller basket, marriage certificate and passport in my cloth handbag, the pouch of Ikeura soil—where did I put it? I checked again and found it at the bottom of the wicker basket.

In the morning Father sat on the cover of the basket and tied it down with sisal. I put on the blue kimono with the Oyama crest.

"Be careful, obey your master, keep up his face, *gaman, gambare,* be patient, persevere," Mother kept repeating. She made me eat an apple so that I could go and return roundly. Then she gave me seven yen in singles. "There's always somebody selling something. You might need something on the ship."

I hugged little brother Toru. "Look after Father and Mother!" I hugged older sister Tomi and her two boys.

The clattering rickshas arrived. Mother rode in one, Father rode the second with the large basket on his lap, and I took the third. The villagers followed on foot.

Uncle Taniguchi, dressed in the same high-collar shirt, vest, and suit, was at the station.

When the train arrived, I bowed deeply to Father and Mother. *"Ishi no ue ni mo gonen!"* I raised my five fingers. "I'll work hard for my master's family for four years, but everything I earn in the fifth year will be for you. I'll go to Hawaii and raise my master's banner."

Father smiled. "You're talking like a samurai."

"Forget the samurai talk," Mother said. "Persevere like a peasant."

I bowed to the sea of faces and shouted to drown out the tremor in my voice, "Thank you for all the favors you've done me and my family! I shall never forget them! I shall be back in five years!"

"Five years even on a rock!" they chorused.

I blushed. They must've thought I was bragging. "To persevere for *three* years even on a rock" was what the proverb said. The *five* just stuck in my head. I was going to be back in five years.

The whistle sounded and I hurried on board. Uncle Taniguchi followed with my basket on his shoulder.

4 · Arrival

We left the basket at a hotel and rode the same rickshas to the immigration office. There was a long line of brides in bright kimonos. Their matchmakers were in dark suits or black *hakama*. The line moved briskly. An official took my papers and copied from my passport, then signed, sealed, and pasted the permit to the passport.

"*Hai,* you're on your way," he said, handing it to me.

Was that it? I'd expected more lines and what the villagers called "the stink of bureaucrats."

"Come, I'll show you Nagasaki," Uncle Taniguchi said when we got outside.

"Aren't you tired?"

He slouched more than usual. Like most men, he didn't talk much. His sister, my mother-in-law, also had a mysterious illness, Grandmother Oyama had said. Mother had said Uncle Taniguchi was squandering the fortune amassed by his father. He contributed heavily to Tenrikyo Church, which promised to cure him of his chronic fatigue.

Hakata is flat, while Nagasaki is bluffs rising from the bay. Hakata was where the samurai repelled the Mongols, while Nagasaki was where the Tokugawa government killed off all the Christians except the *kakure*s. Hakata is Japanese, Nagasaki international. The bay carves the city into a horseshoe, and the buildings are crowded into the small flatland. I gawked at the Western-style houses, the automobiles, the tall white men and their women in body-hugging dresses, and the shops displaying marvelous foreign goods. I looked down at the emerald bay dotted with islets of pine. "It's like a picture postcard," I said.

We arrived an hour early at the pier the next day, and at noon Uncle Taniguchi led me up the gangplank. I showed the white officer my passport and exit permit, and the Japanese steward took us to a small, dark cabin below deck. Two bunk beds were against each wall, leaving a narrow aisle in the middle.

Uncle Taniguchi put the basket under the first bunk on the right.

"It's safer on the bottom. Put something on it."

"Yes." I put my *haori* on the lower bunk.

We went back on deck to watch the others embark, each bride accompanied by her matchmaker. Our parents couldn't afford the train fare and overnight stay in Nagasaki.

When the alarm sounded, I bowed. "Uncle, thank you so much for all the kindness you have shown me and my family."

"Have a nice voyage, Sawa-chan," he said. "Elder sister is fortunate to have such a wise daughter-in-law."

The ship weaved its way around the pine-covered islets. It was so large and sturdy, I needn't have worried about getting seasick.

It was like the first day at kindergarten. We were a bevy of chirping, chattering sparrows. Except now there were no teachers to restrain us! Supper was snapper and rice. The Chinese cooks kept plying us with rice—"*Sukosh mo gohan, ne?*" Their broken Japanese sent us into peals of laughter. We were laughing brazenly with open mouths.

We docked at Yokohama the next morning.

"What is it?" everybody asked about the large, orange-like fruit at breakfast. "It's a grapefruit," the steward said. "You sprinkle sugar on it. Try it. You live seventy-five days longer for every new food you eat."

"I hope I'm not in pain during my last seventy-five days!" Misae at our table said, and everybody guffawed. It would've been unmannerly to laugh like this back home.

We took on fifty more brides at Yokohama and steamed out of Tokyo Bay the next day. We stood at the stern, staring at the gray mist for a glimpse of Mt. Fuji. "It has to be a very clear day," somebody said. We watched till Japan became a dot on the horizon and then disappeared altogether.

On the third day Misae, who was in the bunk across me, undid her pompadour. "My scalp is killing me!" she said. I was going to keep mine no matter how much it itched. Suddenly everybody was saying, "Did you hear? . . ." There were three brides on board who could do the married woman's coiffure. They would charge two yen ($1). What a relief! Now we all washed our hair and piled it on top of our heads. *I should have learned hairdressing instead of sewing,* I thought. They'd be doing about a hundred heads each, making $100 even before they disembark.

"I think my parents undersold me," Misae said when she came back one evening after supper. "Miyamoto Teruko said her parents got a $1,000 engagement gift. There're quite a few $1,000s on board. Mine was only $300! Damn pikers! I guess they took one look at my photo and said, 'This is where we draw the line.' That's what I get for being fat."

"You're not fat!" I said. *Besides . . . ,* I wanted to say, *I'm skinny, and mine was only $350!*

"It would be just my luck," Misae went on, "to find my master bald and twenty years older than his photo. Don't laugh. It's happened. Nobody would send an old or ugly picture of himself, would he? It's human nature. Like baiting a hook. You catch nothing with a bare hook or a bald head. Some of the brides have turned right around and gone back home. Others married somebody else. But most of them didn't want to upset their parents, so they married the old geezers. What would you do? It's frightening. How could you marry somebody who deceived you? Sawa-chan is lucky. She's marrying her second cousin. And he's young. Show them his photo. . . . Isn't he handsome?"

"You're so lucky," the others said.

Most of them showed their husbands' photos. Yoshiko, who slept above me, would sneak looks at hers.

The steward gave a dance lesson one afternoon in the mess hall. The long tables and benches were pushed to the walls, and he put a waltz on the phonograph. The steward picked a partner and demonstrated 1-2-3, 1-2-3, 1-2-3; then he had us dance with each other.

"I hope this trip never ends," Misae said.

On the fourth day the ship pitched and rolled, and everybody in our cabin got sick except Misae and me. We would bring food for the others. Eating in the deserted mess hall became a sport. The plates would slide back and forth on the long table and we'd chase them back and forth, collapsing with laughter.

When I woke up the seventh day, the pitching had stopped and the air had turned warm. I changed into my cotton robe. I helped Yoshiko-san up the stairs to the mess hall. The next evening Captain Long came into the mess hall and said through the steward, "We shall be docking in Honolulu in three days. Please telegraph your husband to come and meet you. If he lives on the outer islands of Kauai, Maui, Molokai, Lanai, or Hawaii, he has to take an overnight steamer to Honolulu. So telegraph him as soon as possible."

We lined up at the telegraph office. The three hairdressers worked nonstop. I sat with Yoshiko in the mess hall. "You have to eat more to build your strength," I said, and gave her some of my bacon and egg. "Do you have money for your hair?"

She nodded. "Thank you. I'm about the last on the list."

We spotted land on the tenth day. A mountain rose like a mirage from the blue expanse. Then there was another, and a third. I'd never seen mountains so craggy or canyons so deep. Dense growth covered them.

"Thank you, San-O-sama," I said, then thought with a laugh, *This must be out of his jurisdiction. After all, he's only a village deity. He'd probably be made guardian of Munakata County if he were promoted.*

"That's Molokai, where the leper colony is," the steward said, pointing to the left.

Fog-shrouded peaks shot up from the turquoise sea and white surf. The slopes were patterns of embroidered green.

Wahh! . . . I thought, *even their quarantine is a place fit for gods.*

Then we turned the corner and were in calmer waters. The smaller mountains were actually craters, their green-brown slopes cascading like pleated fabric from their crowns.

We stood at the bow, sweltering in our pompadours and bridal kimonos. The air was heavy, the sun scorching. Honolulu looked larger than Nagasaki. Palm trees grew everywhere. Rain clouds sat on the distant peaks. *Things must grow wild in this rain and heat,* I thought. *Money must really grow on trees.*

They called us by the American alphabet. I went back to the cabin and changed into my ordinary kimono. I'd be called on the third or fourth day, they said. Yoshiko Akiyama went on the first day. Misae Kurita went the third day. Her husband was a bonito fisherman from Kauai. "He can't be old if he's a bonito fisherman," I told her. "A man has to be young and strong to haul in bonitos." "I hope you're right," she said. Everybody else was married to a plantation worker.

They called me after lunch on the fourth day. A Chinese crewman carried my wicker basket to an inspection area on the dock piled with other wicker baskets. It felt so strange stepping onto the cushiony earth. My steps bounced.

I stood in a line for the medical examination. Anyone with trachoma would be detained, and consumptives would be sent back, they said.

"Mrs. Oyama." A young woman came out of the office with a clipboard. "Oh, you're Mrs. Isao Oyama. You'll be married at my husband's church. I'm Mrs. Nakamura." She ushered me into the small office.

"Tanomimasu." I bowed. All the signs were good. First the marvelous voyage, now a friend among strangers.

Isao had written that he had become a Christian, and we'd be married in a Methodist church. The American government did not recognize the proxy marriages and required picture brides to be married in a mass ceremony at dockside. But Reverend Morimoto of Kahana had arranged for us to be married at Reverend Nakamura's church in Honolulu.

Dr. Fleming was a tall man in a white smock. He examined my eyes, ears, and throat. Then he put the stethoscope to my back and had me cough.

"You're fine," Mrs. Nakamura said. "Please wait outside."

"Thank you so much."

I waited outside in another line. Then a tall Hawaiian native called out six names. He led us into a small room. Six men sat on a wooden bench across the room. Each wore a dark suit and held a brown felt hat with a round crown. Tanned faces and hands. We sat facing them. The woman beside me peeked at her photo.

I didn't have to check mine. There he was, a headful of wavy hair combed to one side. He had Grandmother Oyama's firm jaw, widow's peak, and evenly spaced eyes, nose, and mouth. He sat erect and proud, like his calligraphy. He looked tall. But all the men looked tall sitting. They had long torsos. Their legs were short. Shiny black shoes.

Isao and I stood up simultaneously when "Oyama" was called. He half-smiled. I bowed. *"Tanomimasu."* He nodded. He was barely taller than me.

We went back and stood in line to have my basket inspected.

"How was the trip?" he asked.

"It was so much fun! We ate bacon and eggs and fish and lots of rice! I ate my first grapefruit! We didn't have to cook or wash dishes! I never felt more spoiled!" I said, and caught myself. Gushing was childish.

"Ahhh!" I felt like dancing when we got outside. They can't send me back now.

Isao stepped out and waved for a one-horse buggy. It was just in that instant, the way he walked and waved, that I caught a glimpse of Uncle Taniguchi.

"Kobayashi Hotel at Aala Park," he told the Japanese driver.

"You must be hungry," he said to me.

"No, I just had lunch on board. But you must be hungry."

"I had some noodles at the lunch wagon."

We went up to what looked like the main street and turned left. Everybody drove on the right. There were the same trolleys as in Fukuoka City. But I'd never seen so many automobiles and different people—Japanese, Chinese, native Hawaiians, and whites.

The Japanese-style building was next to a large park. I recognized some girls from the ship and looked for Yoshiko and Misae. I changed into the kimono with the Oyama crest, and we rode back into town and turned left toward the mountain. On the right were handsome buildings with spacious lawns. The white ladies looked so elegant and cool in their fancy hats, white gloves, and colorful umbrellas. On the left were closely set small wooden buildings like those in Hakata and Nagasaki. Many of them had the same carved wooden signs: a large watch for Emura Watchmaker, a large camera for Takashima Photo Studio. There were Chinese and Japanese grocery stores and noodle shops. *It's like Japan,* I thought. The whites were the descendants of the nobility and rich samurai. The rest of us were the commoners.

Farther up were banana patches.

"Wait for us," Isao told the driver.

The modest wooden building sat back from the street. Hedges of bright red hibiscus. It didn't look like a church. Inside were rows of pews. A low railing and a pulpit at the far end. Reverend Nakamura was in his thirties, dressed in a white shirt and tie. He and his two witnesses had been expecting us. He led us into his office, put on his coat, married us, signed the marriage certificate, and gave it to Isao. That was it? Back home everything was so elaborate, everything meticulously recorded, and the dead duly notified. Here it was like a handshake.

"How was the trip?" Reverend Nakamura asked over tea and cake.

"It was like a dream."

"You didn't get seasick?"

"No, I was one of the few who didn't."

"Ah, there must be some fisherman's blood in you. How do you like Hawaii so far?"

"There's so much to see!"

"You can take in only so much at a time," he laughed. He had a softness. I guess he was free of the rituals that made the Buddhist and Shinto priests seem so formal and stiff.

"We have to be going; I have the hack waiting," Isao said.

We rode back down to Takashima Studio for our wedding photo. So that's why the men were in their dark suits. But why all the round hats? Isao had left his at the hotel.

"I'll take you sight-seeing," he said when we got out. "I'd like to take you to Waikiki, but it's probably too late."

"Anything is fine."

"Well, I wanted to show it to you. You probably won't have a chance again for a long time."

Five years is not a long time, I nearly said.

"I can show you the rest of the town."

We turned left on the main street. The shadows were longer now and the air cooler. The people on the street wore loose, informal clothes.

Past the heart of the city were swamps, duck ponds, taro patches, and even a rice paddy. Coconut trees bent toward the ocean like magnificent bows.

We got back at dusk and bathed and changed into cotton robes; then Isao had dinner brought to our room.

"Thank you for the enjoyable day. I didn't realize Honolulu was so large."

"Kahana is nothing like it," he said.

"I'm prepared for it."

"You can't imagine it till you've been there."

"I'm ready to persevere."

I ladled rice into his bowl and waited for him to pick up his chopsticks.

"I didn't realize it was so hot and muggy."

"It's hotter in Pepelau."

He was so stiff. Or was it me?

The maid came and took away the dishes.

"What is Kahana like?"

"It's like a desert."

"But there're lots of Japanese there?"

"About a thousand."

"Wahhh . . . that's twenty times the size of Ikeura!"

"There're ten men to one woman, and the camp's in a clearing of red dirt. Every afternoon there's a swirl of wind we call the *akua* wind."

"What's *akua?*"

"The Hawaiian word for ghost."

Why was he so angry? Maybe he hates small talk. Most of them did.

The maid came back and put down the futons.

"Shall we turn in?" he asked.

"Yes, whatever you wish."

"How do you feel?" he asked as he turned off the lights.

"A little tired." I lay back.

Suddenly he got on top of me and kissed me roughly, then fumbled with my belt, pulled down my panties, and entered me. *Itai!* I cried out in silence. Numbness exploded into pain. He thrust and thrust, panting. The pain subsided, and tendrils of pleasure unfurled slowly, slowly, tingling. But suddenly there was the panic of stampeding hooves; his body stiffened and he groaned and heaved. I jerked my head to avoid the vomit, but he kept gasping, his eyes closed. *He's having a convulsion! I need a spoon!* Suddenly he let out a guttural "Arrrrhh"; then his body went limp and he rolled off.

Are you all right? I was about to ask, when he began to snore. I was all sticky inside and out.

I couldn't sleep. I'd been so tense thinking about all the things that could've gone wrong. Now I felt only tiredness and a sense of relief. So this is how they made babies. I'd seen dogs and chickens do it. But I'd thought humans would be more dignified. I thought of Yoshiko, Misae, and the others. How did they feel, submitting to total strangers? I kept seeing flashes of Uncle Taniguchi, Grandmother Oyama, even my own mother in him—the way he tilted his head, the quizzical look, the flick of the wrist, the cheekbones and eyes, the mouth. . . . So strange and yet so familiar. *I know you even if you don't know me,* I said to myself.

PART II   ✳   *1915–1921*

5 · Kahana

He had been almost tender the next morning. He had taken me to Waikiki, and we'd walked on the sand and watched the natives literally stand on the waves. Then we took the overnight steamer to Pepelau.

Maui looked so enchanting in the morning sun. Patchworks of brown and shaded green covered the slopes to the foot of the mountains. There the green and purple peaks shot up into the rain clouds.

"It's beautiful," I said.

"Not close up," he mumbled.

He carried my wicker basket down to the launch, and we rode past the row of waves toward the wharf, its corrugated sheet-iron roof shining in the sun.

Isao motioned for a hackman he knew, and we got on and clopped into town. The ocean was on our left. A line of closely set stores and noodle shops was to our right.

"It's like Togo," I said, pleasantly surprised.

"Kahana is not like this," he said in a scolding voice.

Once out of town, the cane fields came down to the edge of the road. To our left was the ocean. The road curved in and out with the shoreline. After several kilometers, we turned mountainward into the cane field. The horse slowed to a walk. "Giddyap," Mr. Tanabe, the hack driver, said, whipping him. Young trees lined both sides of the road, their silvery bark stained red. Beyond them were the earthen ditches, and then the fields.

The poor horse strained and strained. Suddenly the cane field parted and we came upon rows and rows of whitewashed barracks stained red! They had corrugated sheet-iron roofs and sat on short posts.

"How can you tell them apart?" My voice cracked.

"They're numbered."

They're like pig sties, I wanted to say.

Women came out and bowed. The children came running behind with bare feet. They looked like the urchins of Nagasaki!

The barracks on either side faced the road, each with two verandas—or rather, a veranda partitioned in the middle. Two families must share each building, the partition following the ridge of the roof and onto the veranda. An eight-by-six-meter building became two four-by-six-meter spaces. *That should be enough for us,* I thought.

A dozen women in white aprons crowded around when we stopped. A tarp was stretched over the space between two barracks. Four rows of trestle tables sat under it, their tops covered with oil paper.

Isao introduced his father first.

"Tanomimasu." I bowed.

He had a mustache and eyes that drooped. He was shorter than Isao and not as tanned.

A woman came down the veranda steps, pushing back her disheveled hair. She had my mother's wide cheekbones and bridgeless nose. "This is Mother," Isao said.

The next person looked like Grandmother Oyama. "Kitano-san," Isao said.

She beamed and clasped my hand. "Welcome to Hawaii." Late Grandfather Oyama had got the maid pregnant, and Aunt Kitano was the result.

Then there were the Hawaii-born children: Chiyako, ten; Kingo, eight; and Masako, two. The adults wore zoris, but the children stood about with red-stained bare feet.

Chiyako and Kingo said nothing, but Masako jumped into my arms and turned to her mother. "Mother, you can die now. Elder sister has come from Japan to look after me!"

"Masako!" her father scolded.

"Aren't children terrible?" I cuddled her.

I was reminded of Uncle Taniguchi's sagging shoulders as I watched Mother Haru trudge back into the house. Chiyako and Kingo darted off. The women went back to their chores. Isao paid Mr. Tanabe and carried my basket around the building.

"Where are you going?"

"We're in the back."

It's strange, I thought, entering from the rear. There were several outside stoves of brick and mortar, each under an open structure with a roof. Some of the white-aproned women were already cooking on them.

I bowed. *"Tanomimasu."*

There was no veranda in the back, just the steps to our screen door. Just inside was the kitchen with a small hibachi. You stepped up into the living quarters. A cotton sheet hung on a rope across the room.

"What's that for?" I asked.

"This side is for us."

How awful! I was going to say, but instead said, near tears, "Where does Azumi-san sleep?" Our space was now a mere four by three meters!

"At the single men's housing."

"I never expected anything so primitive," I said.

A fit of coughing startled me. I peeped over the curtain. Mother Haru lay on the futon on the floor.

I got out the black kimono from my wicker basket and knelt beside her.

"I sewed you this with the family crest."

"Thank you," she mumbled. "Oh, you know, tonight Mrs. Antoku will come by and do your hair. She's a professional hairdresser, but she'll do it free since she's from Fukuoka Prefecture."

Aunt Kitano, coming through the screen door, said, "Come, Sawa-chan, let's go bathe. You must be sticky in this heat."

"Ah, Kitano-san, I made you one, too." I handed her the brown kimono without the crest.

"Oh, thank you," she said. "This is much too good for Kahana."

"What's wrong with Mother?" I asked as we walked up to the bathhouse.

"Nobody knows. Not even the doctors."

The Chinese lived in the upper part of the camp, Aunt Kitano explained as we walked past their barracks. They were all bachelors, and they opened businesses in town as soon as their contracts expired. A large building of corrugated sheet iron sat just past the Chinese camp.

A machine on monstrous rear wheels, a blast of fire in its belly, sat on the other side of the bathhouse.

"What's that?!"

"It's a steam plow. They use it to heat the water when the heater's out of order."

We undressed and descended into what seemed like an enormous underground cavern. A smell of soap and steam oozed from the concrete walls. The bathtub was a small concrete pool. A wooden partition that didn't go all the way to the bottom separated us from the men's side.

"You have to bathe early," Aunt Kitano said. "By eight o'clock there's a gray scum on the water. It's the men. They jump right in without washing, and their scum comes over to our side."

"Maybe it's the Chinese."

"Two dozen Chinese can't produce that much scum."

"But the Japanese are supposed to be clean and considerate."

"Not here."

Mrs. Antoku was waiting when I got back. Isao's younger brother, Kisata, had come with several of his classmates. He was a boarder at Pepelau Technical High School. He had worked for three years, and when the third son, Azumi, arrived in 1913, he was allowed to go to school, and Azumi took his place in the fields. Azumi was also there, bathed and dressed after a day in the fields.

"Here, I wrote a speech for you." Isao handed me a piece of paper.

"You want me to memorize this?"

"Can you?"

"I can't," I cried. "I'll forget! I'll black out!"

Aunt Kitano, who had changed into her new kimono, came in.

"Why don't you read it?" she said. "Keep it in front of you, and if you forget, read it. That's what most people do."

"Is that all right?" I asked Isao.

He nodded.

After Mrs. Antoku put up my hair, Aunt Kitano helped me with the kimono and obi.

"When does it start?"

"As soon as it gets dark," Aunt Kitano said.

Beyond the screen door the sun was setting. The sky turned bright red. In a few minutes it was pitch black.

"Are you ready?" Isao asked, dressed in his black suit.

The party was to last three nights. Saturday night was for the men, Sunday for the women, and Monday for the help. Over a thousand guests! We had less than a hundred at the Ikeura party. *They're so rich, my parents should've asked for $1,000!* I thought.

It wasn't real. Naked bulbs were strung overhead. The men sat on both sides of the long tables. There were mounds of sushi, red fish on large Imari plates, clear white sashimi on beds of lettuce, fish cakes, tempura, fried noodles, pork cutlets, chicken sukiyaki, beer, and *sake*.

Father Takao gave a long speech without any notes. Then Isao stood up. Like his father, he was a born speaker—so calm, even witty.

Finally it was my turn. I stood up and my head wobbled, my hands shook, and I forgot all the words. I grabbed the speech Isao had written. The words were a jumble of chicken footprints! I stood there, unable to raise my head. They were all staring at me! *Please, San-O-sama—I can't faint now!*

I raised five fingers and shouted, "*Ishi no ue ni mo gonen!* Five years even on a rock! The proverb says 'three years,' but I'm prepared to persevere for five years. Even a cold rock would get warm if you sat on it for five years."

Everybody exploded with laughter. Some applauded.

I wasn't trying to be funny. I was only trying to illustrate the proverb, and it came out funny. I picked up Isao's speech and read, "People of Kahana, thank you for all the kindness you have shown me and my family. My aunt Kitano came here in 1889, Father and Mother in 1902, my master and his younger brother, Kisata, in 1910, and the third son, Azumi, in 1913. So I come not as a stranger, but as one with roots here. I will do my utmost to be of service and benefit to the community and repay the kindess you have shown me and my family. *Tanomimasu.*"

I sat down, flushed. I'd done it again, turning stage fright into boasting.

"Well done," Aunt Kitano said. She supervised the serving women and cooks.

Mother Haru, dressed in her new kimono, stayed for the speeches, then went back into the house.

I went into the house at about nine o'clock to change into my powder-blue kimono. Mother Haru coughed.

"I'm sorry you're not feeling well," I said over the curtain.

She lay still. "I'm sorry I can't be of any help."

"It's such a big party. Do they do this for all the brides?"

"No, it was Father's idea. He wanted it to be the biggest."

"Oh, why?"

"That's the way he is. He's showy."

Well, it's nice to have the money to do so, I was going to say. Instead I said, "Excuse me" and went out.

The carousing went on and on past midnight, past one, past two. They drank so much and got so noisy. *It must be the tropics,* I thought. *You drink more.* Besides, being so rich, they never ran out of *sake* and beer.

I felt euphoric. A cool breeze blew down from the mountain. If they were so rich, we'd be returning in less than five years.

I actually enjoyed the next two nights. I didn't panic when I got up. It was like talking to just one person.

We quit by eight o'clock on Monday night, and we had the tarp down and the tables dismantled and stacked against the building by eleven.

Isao was snoring when I lay down beside him. He had had a week's leave. Tomorrow was work. Tomorrow I would begin my real life.

6 · Tofu and Pigs

I'd just fallen asleep when somebody began shaking me. "Sawa-chan. Sawa-chan!"

"Dare?"

"Father," said the face flickering behind a lamp. "We have to make tofu."

Tofu? Yes, tofu. He'd quit field work and become a tofu maker. The previous tofu maker had returned to Japan, and Father Takao had bought the equipment.

I followed him out. It was pitch black beyond the light cast by the kerosene lamp.

"Where are we going?"

"To the tofu shed."

"What time is it?"

"Three."

I stumbled after him, rubbing my arms.

"Mother used to help me," he said.

A large electric grinder, wooden boxes of various sizes, and empty five-gallon cans crammed the small room. He had soaked the beans the night before. We had made tofu in our kitchens back in our village. "Fish of the mountains," we'd called it. This was commercial. We cooked and ground the beans, then separated the juice from the hulls through a cheesecloth bag pressed down by a lever, then added the *nigari*, which separated the hot soy milk into curds and whey. Then we ladled the curd into the wooden settling boxes.

"It'll be firm by daylight," Father Takao said after we had transferred the curd into a box full of tap water.

Back at the barracks he showed me how to fix Isao's and Azumi's lunches. The rice had sat overnight in water in the iron pot with a wooden lid.

We made miso soup while the rice cooked on the stove outside. I woke up Isao and put away our futon, and Father Takao brought out a low round table. Then Azumi arrived in his blue work clothes and straw hat, and the men sat on the floor for a breakfast of rice and miso soup while I packed two lunch pails with rice and braised dried mackerel and filled the canteens.

"You can go back to bed," Father Takao whispered afterward and went to his side of the curtain.

I put away the table and put down our futon once more and fell asleep. I woke up with baby Masako snuggled against me.

The next breakfast was more leisurely.

"Come, let's go sell the tofu," Father Takao said. He pushed the cart up to the shed. The Noguchis were the other tofu makers in camp, but they couldn't compete with us, he said. Mr. Noguchi worked in the fields all day. His wife worked with an infant strapped to her back. Theirs was a manual grindstone, and they made their tofu in their kitchen. They produced only one-fifth of our five dozen cakes a day.

"But we can't dawdle. We have to start a good two hours ahead of Mrs. Noguchi."

He cut the tofu underwater and stacked the cakes into five-gallon cans filled with water. Then he loaded the four cans onto the cart, and we went out on the dusty road. "Tofu, fresh tofu!" he hawked.

Two cakes sold for 5 cents. He recorded each sale in his notebook. It was the grandest party Kahana had seen, everybody said, and we thanked them for their gifts.

"You do it now," he said.

"Tofu! Fresh tofu!"

"Louder."

I hated it. Back home we looked down on merchants. They bought cheap and sold high and produced nothing.

"Go on, say it."

"Tofu, fresh tofu!"

It took two hours to cover the Japanese camp. We sold three and one-half dozen.

"Let's go collect the pig swill now," he said. All tofu makers kept pigs so that they could feed them the protein-rich hulls and whey.

"How many pigs do we have?"

"Fifty."

"Fifty?!"

"Well, twenty are piglets and four are sows."

We pushed the cart now loaded with four dirty pig-swill cans.

"There are thirty families from Fukuoka Prefecture, plus another thirty who give us their swill, so we collect twenty each day, ten in the morning and ten in the afternoon."

The swill cans were hung on nails outside the kitchens. Father Takao emptied the first few cans into our five-gallon cans and said, "Now you do it." Once the cans were full we pushed the cart to the tofu shed and added some hulls and whey to the swill.

The row of pigpens was downhill on the lower boundary of the camp. We rented seven pens. Their concrete floors sloped into the four-foot-wide irrigation ditch. Beyond it were the cane fields.

He showed me how to dump the swill into the troughs, the bigger amount going to the piglets and smaller pigs. The stink was over-powering. Pigs are finicky; they don't eat where they defecate. We kept them in open pens back home. Now they stepped on the squishy green-gray feces as they ate.

"The pens have to be washed every day, but we do it every other day," Father Takao said. "Here, I'll show you." He turned on the faucet to the long hose and climbed into the first pen in his wooden clogs. He hosed the feces from the back and between the pigs' legs into the ditch. "You have to do it while they're eating. I use the broom every other time."

It was half past eleven when we got back, and Chiyako and Kingo had come home for lunch from Kahana Grade School. After I'd washed the dishes, Father Takao said, "Come, let's go cut some *hono hono* grass." He got a couple of barley bags and a hoe, and he pushed the same cart into the cane fields. The reddish-green tubular grass grew on the banks of the irrigation ditches beside the roads. You cut the root and got a spread of a couple feet in diameter.

Father Takao then taught me how to boil the grass in a twenty-gallon galvanized iron tub. "The pigs need this change of diet twice a week," he said. Afterward we collected swill from ten more families, added the grass, and fed the pigs their supper. By then it was five o'clock, and Isao was home from the fields. He worked from 5:45

A.M. to 4:30 P.M. with fifteen minutes for breakfast and thirty minutes for lunch.

I cooked supper, and Chiyako helped with the dishes. Then Mother Haru asked me to comb her hair. She sat on a stool while I combed her tresses and bundled them in the back.

"It feels good. It's something I can look forward to, now that you're here. Oh, there's some sewing for the children I left for you. It'll be easier once I get stronger," she said. "Oh, the laundry. Isao's and Azumi's work clothes have to be boiled once a week in lye soap to get out the dirt. The family laundry has to be done once a week also."

The last day of the month was payday. Isao came home at half past five with a $10 gold coin in a small brown envelope. He had worked only sixteen days. It amounted to 62.5 cents a day. Was that all? Where was all the money that grew on trees?

Isao explained that he would've made $16.25 if he'd worked twenty-six days.

Isao gave his pay to his mother, who gave him $3 in allowance.

"Why don't you ask for more? There're two of us now."

He shrugged.

"Do you want me to?" I asked.

"No!"

Chiyako, Kingo, and I went to collect the money for the tofu that evening. I hated handling money. Besides, I felt bad interrupting people's supper. Most bills amounted to $1.50 for the month, but some families could only pay half. "Oh, all right, I'll carry it over to next month," I said. A couple families owed as much as $5. But it pleased me that they paid even a little. It showed sincerity. We collected $27.25.

"It should be $38.45," Mother Haru huffed. "You should not let them off so easily. We have our expenses, too. More than half of what we collect is for expenses. You should insist next time. Our store in Japan would've collapsed if we'd been so soft."

I couldn't sleep, thinking of what Grandmother Oyama had said in the bath the night of the wedding party back home. She'd sounded so serene, picking apart her number one son, Father Takao. Takao had promised to return in five years, and it was now thirteen years. As number one son, he'd inherited the farm. It was his duty to care for her in her old age. It was too bad Saburo, the third born, wasn't the number one son; he was brighter and more ambitious.

36

So why this lavish party for me? It must've cost $800. He could've done it for half. "He's showy," Mother Haru had said. But it's unconscionable to put up such a big face just for show when you're making only $16.25 a month and 5 cents for two cakes of tofu.

7 · I am Not a Thief!

Three dollars a month allowance didn't last two weeks. On Sundays Masako would lie between us. "Elder sister, elder brother, will you please buy me a donut?" So we'd send Chiyako or Kingo to Kanda Bakery and Restaurant near the bathhouse for seven jelly-filled donuts.

One day while collecting her pig swill, Aunt Kitano said, "Here, I made this for you." It was a gold wedding band. She'd given Mr. Yoneda a $10 gold piece and paid him a couple of dollars to pound it into a ring.

"Oh, thank you so much, Kitano-san! It fits just right."

"Isn't it beautiful?" I showed it off at supper. They all glanced at it and looked away. *I just wanted to share my joy; I didn't mean to embarrass you,* I wanted to say.

Collecting pig swill gave me the chance to meet people. Mrs. Kuni was a widow with four children. She supported her family with the Kuni Barbershop and Candy Store. She was also from Fukuoka Prefecture. "Everybody says you're the hardest working bride in Kahana," she said one day.

"Well, Mother is sick."

"Yes, that's one reason . . ."

Doing the laundry was also fun, especially when Mrs. Shiotsugu was there. The plantation provided the slab of concrete, six faucets, and washtubs cut from wooden barrels. We brought our own soap and washboards. We were all so reserved except for Mrs. Shiotsugu, who loved to talk. She called Mother Haru, Aunt Kitano, and Mrs. Kuni the "the big three."

"Actually it's the 'big two' since Mrs. Oyama is absent most of the time. Even then it's impossible to know whom to obey when both of them are giving orders," she'd say. She'd reply with a military *"Hai! Hai!"* Afterward she would explain, "They're the feudal lords, and we're the vassals." Then she'd repeat the story of her first meeting with her husband. "You can imagine my shock! I looked at the photo and stared at him! I looked," she said, looking at her palm, "and stared again! He was bald as a melon! The photo showed a bushy head of hair! I stooped down and said, 'You're not Shiotsugu-san, I hope?'" It never failed to trigger an explosion of laughter. I thought of Misae on the *Tenyo Maru*. I envied Misae and Mrs. Shiotsugu. They felt no shame in baring their family secrets. They could make fun of themselves and their secrets and make people laugh.

Aunt Kitano always looked after me. "Why don't you take the hose to your right, Nakata-san. That way, Sawa-chan could use your hose." A short hose made from denim was attached to each faucet. Whenever I was frantic, she'd say, "Don't hurry, Sawa-chan; let your other chores wait."

"Why don't you work in the fields? It's a lot easier. You have a definite schedule then," the working brides said.

One afternoon in mid-November I came home from collecting pig grass. Chiyako and Kingo were at Reverend Morimoto's language school. Mother Haru called me. She sat on the stool beyond the curtain.

"Money's been missing from the bowl," she muttered.

"Oh, how much?"

"Over $3."

"Hmmm. . . . Did I miscount the tofu receipts?"

"Somebody's been taking it."

"Been? Not only once?"

"Don't act so innocent."

"What are you saying?"

"You've been taking it."

"You're accusing me of stealing?"

"You take 25 cents at a time, hoping I wouldn't notice."

"I didn't take a cent!"

"It never happened before you came."

"You probably mislaid it!"

"How could I mislay it so many times? You've been taking it."

"No, I haven't." I hurried out.

I felt like bawling, but the pig grass had to be cooked, more swill collected, and the pigs fed; then the rice, tofu, vegetables, and *iriko* washed and cooked.

At supper Mother Haru scolded Isao for spending so much time with his church activities. When I ladled the rice into Chiyako's bowl and proffered it, she yanked it with one hand. *It's just an accident,* I thought. Then she did it again. And a third time. *What's the matter?* I looked to Mother Haru and Father Takao to chastise her. They didn't notice, or pretended not to. Masako was still unspoiled, but both Chiyako and Kingo were so ill-mannered. They looked so dirty with their bare feet, and they darted off every time I tried to befriend them. They spoke to each other in a burst of gibberish, which didn't sound at all like Captain Long's melodious English. *It must be the tropics,* I thought. *Discipline is the first thing to go.*

That night I quit the ironing early and turned in as soon as Isao did.

"Mother accuses me of stealing from the petty cash bowl. I didn't do it."

"She must've misplaced it," he said.

"She swears she didn't. She says I took it because it never disappeared before. It's outrageous! I never dreamed in my wildest dreams I'd be accused of stealing!"

He nodded in the dark.

"Will you say so to her?"

"Hmmm." He nodded.

"But I want you to talk to her."

"Hmmmm."

The next week 25 cents disappeared, and then another 25 cents.

"Why don't you hold on to the money yourself? Nobody can take it then," I said.

"You can't make us change our ways. You have to change *your* ways."

"I didn't take it!" I burst out crying.

I overheard her telling Isao, "You have to reform her. It's shameful to have a thief in the house. She's so brazen, she does it right under my nose."

"I didn't take the money!" I said whenever we were alone. "You have to believe me. She's mistaken or lying."

"Why would she lie?"

"I don't know. Maybe to persecute me."

"Why would she want to persecute you?"

"I don't know. Maybe she's angry because I cost so much—the boat fare, engagement gift, the party. Even the kimonos. The silk cost so much. I'll pay her back. I work sixteen hours. I hardly sleep while she sleeps all day!"

"I don't want to talk about it!"

"But you must!"

"Shut up!"

I remembered all the proverbs. "Train the bride when she first arrives"; "Don't feed the bride autumn eggplant or autumn mackerel"; "A bad wife is fifty years of bad crops"; "Brides and mothers-in-law are like dogs and monkeys"; "Yesterday's bride is today's mother-in-law." But they were about other people. I was family. Even Chiyako turned into the proverbial "thousand devils." She spied on me and reported to Mother Haru, "Elder sister was burning a letter at the stove and crying" or, "Elder sister was at the cane field, crying." Late at night I would sneak out beyond the pigpens. The cane was short, and the vast dark ocean sat below. I wept as I faced Molokai. This was the direction from which our ship had come. I had not written my parents since the first week. "How are you?" "What's happening?" they kept writing.

✳ ✳ ✳

Aunt Kitano laughed her deep laugh. "How much is involved? 25 cents a week? She's probably miscounting."

"But it's been happening for a month now. Every week she blames me. I can't stand it."

"What does younger brother say?"

"Father doesn't say anything. He just sips his *sake*."

The next day Aunt Kitano visited us after supper and invited Isao and me for supper on Sunday.

"If it's all right with you?" I turned to Mother Haru.

"Well, Chiyako and I will have to fix supper," she mumbled.

Aunt Kitano's husband was ten years younger, but he looked dried up. A color-tinted wedding photo in an oval frame hung on the parlor wall. He had looked so young then, only six years ago. Aunt Kitano hadn't changed—a square, handsome face with dancing eyes.

She had divorced her first husband to marry Mr. Kitano. All the children went with the husband in such cases, and the new husband paid all their boat fare back to Japan.

Aunt Kitano fixed chicken sukiyaki, which she called *heka,* on her hibachi. It was so pleasant, the smell of soy and sugar filling the spacious room, eating food somebody else had cooked. Mr. Kitano hardly said anything, but Aunt Kitano talked excitedly of the old days when Kahana was a treeless expanse of red dirt. Twenty-five hundred people were crowded into shacks. The barracks came later. In those days the *akua* winds stained your wash as soon as you hung it out to dry.

"It still does!" I said. "I was near tears the first time it happened!"

"But we had to do it two to three times. Can you imagine a place without trees? The wind came up every afternoon."

✳ ✳ ✳

"Let's not go home; it's early yet," I said to Isao afterward.

"It's half past nine."

"Let's go to the park." There was a park below the plantation store.

I sat on the swing. "I had such a nice time. Did you?"

After a while he said, "I have to go to work tomorrow."

"Can we get a house to ourselves? The Yabuis and Shiotsugus have their own houses."

"I don't think so."

"Why not?"

"Who's to help Mother?"

"We can find one nearby. She won't keep accusing me of stealing if we move out."

"We can't."

"Why not?"

"Can't you hear what I'm saying? When I say, 'We can't,' we can't!"

I blurted out the old proverb, "A lifetime of happiness or misery is in the hands of a stranger."

"Nani?"

"Nothing." I wondered what else Misae or Mrs. Shiotsugu would have said.

The next morning Mother Haru asked me to comb her hair.

"Can it wait till later? I've got so much to do."

"No, I want to talk to you now."

"You shouldn't make Mrs. Kitano your model," she said as soon as I let down her hair.

"What do you mean?"

"She can't ever return to Japan."

"Why not?"

"Why not? She fell in love with Mr. Kitano, who's addicted to gambling. She left her husband and five children. Eloping with her first husband was bad enough. She begged her first husband to leave their youngest child with her, but he refused. I don't blame him."

My hands shook so much I stopped the combing. I shouldn't let her upset me so. She's so calm, and I'm quaking. But I can't lose to her! "She treats me like a mother," I squeaked.

"She's transferring her love for Sadao to you."

"Who's Sadao?"

"Her youngest, the one she wanted to keep. One more thing—she and her first husband loaned us $80 for our boat fare in 1902. They never told us they were getting $50 from the plantation for every new laborer they recruited. They should have knocked off $25 at least. Even we pawnbrokers are not that usurious . . ."

I let her talk on and on while I kept my squeaky voice to myself and imagined jabbing her with the sharp end of the comb.

8 · A Dog-and-Monkey Fight

It was my first New Year's in Hawaii! *Mochi, ozoni, soba;* all the cooking and sweeping had to be done by midnight on the thirty-first. We grew a year older. But instead of sea bream we had the brilliant red *onaga,* cooked whole for good luck.

Isao went calling with Kawai Ichiro and others from the Methodist young men's club. He and Mr. Kawai took turns being president. They made a strange pair. Mr. Kawai was a gangly five feet eight inches whereas Isao was small with bird-like quickness. Father Takao had acted as matchmaker for Mr. Kawai's marriage to a nisei woman.

New Year's day was on a Saturday. On Monday we still had thirty cakes of tofu left over from Friday.

"Just wash them and put them in fresh water," Father Takao said.

"We can't sell these. They're slimy," I protested.

"Let's see." He examined a cake. "They're fine."

I sniffed at another. "It even smells rancid."

"They won't know the difference."

"How can you say that?!"

"But we can't throw them away."

"What if we donated them to the temple?"

"They'll never know."

"Even a child knows when a tofu is rancid! We can fool them once, but they'll never buy from us again!"

"Hmmm . . . maybe you're right," he said. "We'll donate them to the temple. Besides, I doubt if they need tofu today. They're still feasting on leftovers."

Soon after New Year's day Mother Haru was hospitalized for several days in Dr. Tofukuji's private hospital in Wailuku. "Another 50 cents is missing!" she said as soon as she got home.

"Why would I steal? I have no place to spend it."

"You're sending the money to Japan!"

"Why would I do that?"

"Your family is bankrupt!"

"So is the Oyama family!"

"But you're more interested in helping them."

"Why don't you check my basket?" I said. I kept my personal things in the wicker basket I'd brought from Japan.

"I did."

"Did you find the money there?"

"It doesn't mean a thing."

"Why don't you go to the store and check?!" I said. The plantation store sold money orders.

"I did."

"So what did you find out?"

"It doesn't mean a thing. You could be hiding it in the cane fields. You go there late at night."

"I go there to cry. I feel so ashamed, I can't even write my parents." I walked off. I had so much to do, I had no time to stop and cry.

"You look tired. Are you all right?" Mrs. Kuni asked one day when I went to collect her swill. Her husband had died of a ruptured appendix several years ago, and she'd gone back to Japan with his ashes and her two sons. She now supported her four children with her barbershop and candy store. The plantation forbade her to sell groceries, which the plantation store monopolized.

I felt like spilling everything, but you never talked of family business with outsiders.

"You've grown thinner," Mrs. Kuni said. "Is everything all right? Everybody says you're the hardest working bride in Kahana. It must be difficult having Haru for a mother . . ."

"It's probably because she's so sickly. . . . She finds fault in everything."

"They do it deliberately!" Mrs. Kuni said. "They think humiliation builds character!" She talked about the time she went back to

Japan with her husband's ashes. Her in-laws gave a party at a tea-house. They had her two boys enter, the younger first. They all stood up and shouted, "Banzai! Banzai! Banzai!" The older boy got the same three banzais. But when she entered, there was dead silence! All forty faces didn't even turn to look at her! "Can you imagine the humiliation? I'll never get over it till the day I die! They must think you have to mistreat a daughter-in-law to make her a better mother!"

❋   ❋   ❋

"Has the money turned up?" Aunt Kitano asked several days later.

"No, it keeps disappearing and she keeps accusing me."

"She's getting senile. If not, somebody is actually taking it."

"She's not senile. She's sharp."

"She's so useless. She can't even earn her own keep. Younger brother married her for her dowry and now he spends everything on her doctor's bills. She can't go to the plantation doctor like the rest of us. She needs a specialist in Wailuku. It costs $4 just for the hack fare."

"What's wrong with her?" I asked, remembering her younger brother, Uncle Taniguchi, and his chronic fatigue. He had donated most of the family fortune to Tenrikyo Church, which had promised to cure him of his mysterious illness.

"I think it's neurasthenia."

"What is that?"

She shrugged. "Nervous exhaustion."

"Is there no medicine for it?"

"I don't know." She paused. "What does Takao say about the missing money?"

"Nothing."

"And your husband?"

"He says he believes me, but then Mother is always at his other ear."

"You know, younger brother is not as honest as he pretends to be. When he first got here, he never told anybody he'd left three sons and a daughter in Japan. When Kingo was born, he threw a party fit for a number one son. The villagers brought expensive gifts. How can you lie knowing you'll be found out? Or maybe he never intended to send for your husband. When Isao did come, he pretended the celebration

46

for Kingo never happened. He must think other people have no memory. You know why he hasn't returned to Japan?"

"Because he hasn't been able to save enough?"

"That, of course. But he enjoys it here. He can act the village headman. People come to him for their letters. They love his calligraphy. He'd be a nobody in Japan."

It rained continually in February. I would slip and stumble, pushing the cart up to the tofu shed. The road in front of our barracks became a quagmire. Mother Haru seemed extra tired, but she didn't let up.

"I didn't take it," I countered each time.

One night Isao was awake when I turned in. Whenever he'd waited up before, it had been for sex.

"Mother's been nagging me and nagging me to get you to confess," he said in the dark.

"How can I confess to something I haven't done!? You really don't believe me, do you? You really think I'm a thief, don't you?"

"Shhh."

"Let her hear! Nothing's private in this house anyway!"

"I just want some peace and quiet."

"Then you have to convince her. Tell her I'm too honest. I could not steal even if ordered to do so."

"I can't stand it. I get an earful from both of you!"

"You have to believe me!"

"I don't want to talk about it."

"But we have to talk about it."

"I've worked ten hours. I'm tired."

You work ten hours and you act like you returned from battle with the prized head of the enemy! I wanted to say, but instead I said, half-crying, "I work sixteen hours seven days a week and I'm accused of stealing!"

"I told you I don't want to talk about it!"

"But don't you care what happens to me?"

"Shut up!"

"But you must tell her!"

"Yakamashii!"

He turned around and was asleep in a few minutes. He could escape so easily. It took me forever to fall asleep. But I felt good. I was sure Mother Haru had heard every word.

She kept up her mumbling at supper. "There's a mouse in the

house who loves 25-cent pieces." "We're never going to save any money with 25 cents disappearing every week." "We've lost $10 already."

"I never stole a penny in my life!" I shot back.

It was a woman's fight—of dog versus monkey. The others stayed uninvolved except Chiyako, who kept yanking away her bowl of rice. Father Takao sat above it all, sipping his *sake*. Isao and Azumi gobbled down their food and ran. I chewed and chewed, forcing myself to swallow. *I have to keep up my strength*, I thought.

Aunt Kitano laughed. "That's the trouble with moneylenders. It enrages them when they feel they're being cheated out of a penny."

The first Sunday in March was glorious. The rain had stopped, and the air and sky were so bright they hurt your eyes. Isao went to the language school, which became the Methodist church on Sundays. When he didn't come home for lunch, we assumed he'd gone to Kawai Ichiro's for lunch. But then he didn't come home for supper.

Azumi said, "People at the single men's housing saw him walking down the hill early this morning."

"Did you see him?" Father Takao asked.

"No, but Watanabe told me."

"What was he wearing?" Father Takao asked.

"His Sunday school clothes," I said.

"He must've just gone to Pepelau on some business," Mother Haru grumbled. "He should have told us."

When he didn't show up by ten, Father Takao shrugged. "He'll be here by tomorrow morning."

There was no sign of him when I awoke at three. I went to the tofu shed and cooked the beans that had been soaked overnight. Then I ground and strained them and let the mash set. Back at the barracks I cooked the rice and the miso soup, folded our futons, brought out the low table, and woke up Father Takao. "Isao-san hasn't come home."

"He's run away again." Mother Haru dragged herself to join us.

When Azumi arrived from the single men's housing, Father Takao told him to go look for him. "I'll tell the *luna*," Father Takao said.

All morning long I kept thinking, *Maybe he's looking for another job in Pepelau. It'd be so nice to live there.*

Azumi returned at lunchtime. "People saw him getting on the launch at the wharf and boarding the steamship," he mumbled.

"Where would he go?" Mother Haru said.

48

Azumi shrugged. "Honolulu?"

"Where in Honolulu? He doesn't know anybody," Mother Haru said.

"He probably went to Kobayashi Hotel," I offered. "That's where we stayed. It was next to a large park with a stream beside it."

"Aala Park," Father Takao said.

"Where did he get the money? Don't tell me *he's* been taking it!" Mother Haru frowned.

"Don't be silly!" I cried.

"Where did he get the money, then?"

"He could have borrowed it from Mr. Kawai. And he still had the $3 allowance," I said.

"When's the next boat?" Father Takao asked.

"Tomorrow," Azumi mumbled.

"Get on it," Father Takao said.

"And keep it quiet. This is family business," Mother Haru whispered.

Azumi laughed. "Heh-heh."

"You understand?" she asked.

Azumi shrugged. "Everybody knows already. I had to ask around to find out."

"Well, don't tell them any more than you have to," she muttered.

"Heh-heh," he laughed.

I went through the chores in a daze: making tofu, making breakfast, hawking tofu, collecting swill and feeding the pigs. . . . What's next? Yes, lunch. . . . Then it was a supper of rice and miso soup and tofu and pickled cabbage. The routine was a comfort. I stayed up late and finished the sewing and ironing; I put down our futon and lay down, exhausted. But as soon as I closed my eyes, I felt wide awake. *What's the matter with him?* We're taught from infancy to *gaman* and *gambaru*. Patience and perseverence are second nature. I remember my own father saying Isao was undisciplined, wishing I could marry the second son instead.

❋   ❋   ❋

He'd run away before. He was eight when his parents left for Hawaii. "Look after your siblings," Takao had said. Once when a bully beat up Kisata, Isao ambushed the bigger boy with a big stick. The injured boy's parents couldn't get old Mr. Taniguchi to punish

Isao. Better not play with him, the other parents said. At fourteen he was sent to live with his uncle to attend middle school. Grandmother Oyama had talked about it in the bath. Saburo, the most ambitious and brightest of her children, had been adopted into the well-to-do Yamada family. Saburo's wife was so homely they couldn't have married her off except to an adopted husband. It must've galled her to have Isao, a vestige of an Oyama, in the household. It was a *modan* household. The rooms were cluttered with rugs, chairs, sofas, tables, dressers, bookcases, lamps, and knickknacks. The tablecloths, cutwork place mats, embroidered napkins, crochet runners, and antimacassars were kept immaculate.

Isao ran away after a year. He sneaked on trains going to Shimonoseki, stowed away on the ferry, and stole a ride to Togo. It took him seven days. The Yamadas called the police and his grandfather. "Send him back!" Mr. Yamada told Grandfather Taniguchi when Isao showed up. "Why don't I keep him till school reopens? He can work in my store. I need the help," Grandfather Taniguchi pleaded.

In September his grandfather put him on the train to Tokyo. But Isao got off at Hakata and exchanged his ticket for a passage to Pusan, Korea. From there he made his way to Seoul, where his second cousin had a clothing store. "I'll run away again if you send me back," Isao said. His second cousin agreed to hire him for room and board plus spending money. "He doesn't have the perseverance to become a scholar. The hazing at school was probably too much for him," Saburo wrote Takao. Takao had no choice but to send for him. He was to bring his younger brother, Kisata, with him.

Isao was overjoyed. He'd looked after his siblings as his father had asked him to do. He expected a hero's welcome. But his parents considered him a failure. They "feted" him with the usual fare of miso soup, tofu, pickles, dried mackerel, and rice, then sent him and Kisata to work in the fields the next day.

✳   ✳   ✳

He's not a bad man, I thought. He never once made fun of my family. He probably didn't want to get married anymore than I. He was happy being president of the Methodist club. Reverend Morimoto, sixteen years his senior, was like a father. Isao spent many evenings and Sunday afternoons with the reverend and the Methodist club, and he always carried a book he'd borrowed from the reverend.

He kept a busy notebook. "What are you doing?" I asked once. "Oh, writing things—English words, Hawaiian words," he said. He had a good memory and a beautiful hand. He was a scholar despite what his uncle and parents thought. Reverend Morimoto also believed he was a scholar.

Was our nagging so unbearable? But why was Mother Haru so hard on him? Eight-year-old Kingo could do no wrong, but she found fault with everything Isao did. You heard of wives running away from abusive husbands and mothers-in-law or men running away from creditors. But whoever heard of a man fleeing from a dog-and-monkey fight? But he'd run away in Tokyo, too. Homely Mrs. Yamada must've picked on him the way Mother Haru does. What can he do in Honolulu? Whom does he know? What skills does he have? What if something happens to him? What if? . . . All the "what ifs" crowded into my mind.

All the worries were whirring in the dark when the alarm clock jarred me from my stupor.

9 · You Can't Be Too Careful

I'm on the moon, and the only light is from my hurricane lamp. I pull the key string off my wrist and insert the key into the padlock. I grope for the string in the dank room, and a blinding flash explodes the dream.

Cans and boxes are all around. I light the fire under the beans and sit, dozing. I ladle the beans into the grinder and flip the switch. Its noise barely penetrates my cocoon. I sit on the lever to strain the soy milk through the cheesecloth. I nearly doze off, turn, and shriek.

"Good morning." Mr. Yamamoto stood at the doorway, holding up a lamp, a smile on his round face.

"You scared me!" I picked up the lever.

"I'm sorry. I cleared my throat several times. I guess you didn't hear."

"You're up early."

"We water *luna*s have to get up early to open the gates so that the water will get down to the fields by the time the workers get there."

"Oh, do you come this way often?"

He was in his late twenties, a bachelor. He wore a straw hat and blue denim work clothes.

"Sometimes," he said. "Can I help you?"

"No, thank you! You'll be late. Your water won't get to the fields in time." I ladled the milk into the settling boxes.

I was startled by a sudden flurry. He grabbed my buttocks before I could turn! I yelped and swung the ladle. *Pakkak!*

"Excuse me!" I blurted, feeling like a fool.

"I'm sorry." He rubbed his cherubic cheek. "I've been in love with you since the day you came."

"Go find yourself your own wife!"

I held the ladle ready. Next time it wouldn't be backhanded, and there'd be no stupid apology.

"Well, I'll be going then." He nodded and backed out.

"Yes, please do!"

When I locked up and headed home, I felt it hadn't happened. It couldn't happen in broad daylight. The wee hours turned people into barbarians. Nobody was watching. Shame was forgotten. You were on the moon, free of all the daytime constraints.

Had I been too stern? I could understand why wives got fooled so easily. We're starved for attention and praise. But as soon as you hesitated, you got caught in the gossip mill. They whispered hateful lies, like Mrs. Shiotsugu and Aunt Kitano being part-time prostitutes. How could they have known except that the men had boasted. One couldn't be too careful. To be talked about was to be tainted.

The next day I went into the cane fields to collect pig grass. Mr. Nomura, another young bachelor, suddenly appeared out of the tall canes and began helping me. He cut one clump of grass after another with his hoe and carried them to the cart.

"Oh, thank you."

"There're some really big ones inside. I work this field."

"No, this is plenty."

"They're just close by." He grabbed my elbow.

"Cut it out!" I yanked back my arm.

"I'll go get them for you."

"No, thank you! This is plenty!" I filled the barley bags and lifted them onto the cart and pushed off.

Now I was really angry. He was no different than Mr. Yamamoto. Why were they so brazen? They never acted like this back home. It was true what people said—the traveler leaves shame behind.

Nobody was home on Friday morning. Father Takao had taken Mother Haru to Wailuku to see Dr. Tofukuji, Chiyako and Kingo were at school, and Masako was out playing.

I had come home from selling tofu. Suddenly, Isao appeared at the back steps.

"Welcome home." I rushed to the screen door. He looked haggard and unshaven. "Where's Azumi-san?"

"Went back to the single men's housing, I guess," he mumbled, taking off his shoes.

"Were you at Kobayashi Hotel?"

He nodded and pushed past me.

I put away his shoes and watched him change into a clean shirt.

"I told Azumi-san he'd probably find you there. What were you planning to do in Honolulu?"

He shrugged.

"You must've had some idea of how you were going to earn a living."

"I wanted to be a barber or a *naniwa-bushi* reciter."

"Do you have any experience as a barber or a ballad reciter?"

He shook his head.

"Sir, if you wish to become a barber or a *naniwa-bushi* reciter, why don't you train yourself first, and then test your hand? *Ne?* Nobody can succeed without preparation."

"*Baka!*" His hand flashed out and whacked me.

Tears streamed down my cheeks. I couldn't believe it! I'd never been hit in all my life!

"Sir!" I stuck out my jaw. "You cannot do anything on the spur of the moment! Everything takes preparation!"

"Fool!"

"There is no easy way! It takes hard work! You can't run away every time—"

"Shut up!" His hand stunned me again!

"Hit me all you want if it makes you feel better!" I screeched, covering my face.

"Shut up!" he yelled, and walked out.

I crumpled to the floor and bawled. This wasn't happening; I was in a dream, but my cheek burned and throbbed. I cried and cried until the spasms became hiccups.

I have to collect swill, feed the pigs, Chiyako and Kingo will be coming home for lunch . . .

10 · Aunt Kitano

Supper was a wake. We hardly spoke. The gossips must be having a field day. They always whispered, hands over mouths, pretending solicitude.

I got back early the next morning from peddling tofu.

"Will you massage my shoulders before you go out?" Mother Haru asked.

"I'm so behind in my work . . ." Lately, whenever she wanted to lecture me she'd ask me to comb her hair or massage her shoulders.

"Isao is so immature. He's still a boy. You have to be patient with him."

"You should be warmer toward him. You show affection only to Kingo."

"We were so disappointed when he ran away from his uncle's. We wanted him to become somebody. We wasted a whole year of room and board. We're sending money now for Aya's education. She's in middle school. She was only six months old when we left for Hawaii. We had to wait in Yokohama, so I cabled younger sister to bring her to me. I suckled her till we embarked. Younger brother . . . you met him; he was your matchmaker. His wife was nursing her own infant, so we asked her to nurse Aya also. When Father visited them several months later, Aya was skin and bones while her own baby was round as a ball. Father wrote that Aya jumped on his back and wouldn't get off. 'Poppo, poppo, poppo,' she said, imitating the train that had brought her and Father to Kokura. Father brought her back to Togo and fattened her with rice gruel and crushed tofu and fish. I can't forgive younger brother for being so henpecked. He wouldn't have lifted a finger even if his wife had starved Aya to death."

"Isn't it sad how cruel we are to our own kin? We're kinder to strangers."

"She's not kin; she's an outsider," she huffed. "You know, we worried ourselves sick when we were looking for a bride for Isao. Being in Hawaii, we couldn't investigate a prospective bride's family tree. So we decided, why not choose a relative? But a prosperous family would not ship off its daughter as a picture bride no matter how large the engagement gift, so we had to find a relative that . . ." her voice trailed off.

I waited, but she must've figured she'd said too much.

She said instead, "There must've been a thief in the Ito family tree."

"Or maybe in the Oyama tree," I said. This was ridiculous! She was my mother's first cousin. A common ancestor could've been a thief!

"Well, the money never disappeared till you came."

"Mrs. Kuni thinks you're being harsh just to build my character."

"You've talked to Mrs. Kuni? Have you no shame?!"

Not about the money, I was going to say, but instead said, "Well . . . she asked me why I was so thin, so I told her." It wasn't really a lie.

"Who else have you talked to?"

"Kitano-san asked me also, so I told her. I can't keep secrets."

"It's shameful! Family business is family business!"

Talking to outsiders is my only weapon flashed through my mind, but I said, "Aunt Kitano believes me. She thinks you're miscounting or growing senile."

"You have no shame advertising your shame?"

"I didn't steal it. That's why I can talk about it."

"I'm checking the store every fortnight. No matter how much you steal, you won't be able to send it to your parents."

"Please check all you want. You'll only tire yourself."

"Sawa-chan! Sawa-chan!" Aunt Kitano's voice sounded at the veranda.

"*Hai,*" I yelled.

"Oh, I thought you were in the back." She stepped inside.

She wore a pink blouse and a gray-blue skirt and carried a pink flowery parasol. "Come, I'll take you to Pepelau," she said.

"Is it all right, Mother?"

"She can't go. There's too much work to be done," Mother Haru grumbled.

"Work can wait. It won't run away," Aunt Kitano said.

"Who's to do all the work?"

"Who did it before Sawa-chan came?"

"I can't do it."

"Then let it wait. Sawa-chan hasn't had a day's rest since she got here."

"Neither have I!"

"That's a matter between Takao and you. You talk to him. Come on, Sawa-chan, change your clothes."

"Is it all right, Mother?"

"Come on; the chores can wait."

"I'll work extra hard tomorrow." I changed into clean underwear and a fresh cotton kimono.

I bowed. "I'll be going."

I skipped out. The cane tassels danced as we walked down the tar road. The turquoise ocean turned deep blue and rose to meet the aqua-blue sky. Rows of white surf moved in slow motion to the shore. The colors were so intense. The reds of hibiscus, the whites of ginger. The plums and azaleas must be in bloom back home; cherry blossoms would bloom in a few weeks. Aunt Kitano held her parasol over us.

"I can't thank you enough."

"I guess it was too much for Isao. He doesn't realize your lot is ten times worse," she said.

"Well, I shouldn't have complained to him so much. He was getting it from both of us."

"You know, I've been thinking. Somebody must actually be stealing the money. She's not miscounting or forgetting. She wouldn't persist if she were just trying to discipline you. She doesn't have the energy. So somebody *must* be taking it."

"But who?"

"Chiyako?"

"She follows me everywhere and reports everything I do to Mother."

"Kingo?"

"He's only eight—no, he's nine now."

"Masako is . . ."

"Three."

"Azumi?"

"He works all day. The money disappears during the day."

"That leaves younger brother."

"But why would Father have to steal? He goes to the store and buys everything on credit."

"You know, they made him manager of the plantation store when he got here. He had two years of business school and could read and write English. But they fired him after a year. He claimed it was because he'd extended credit to those the plantation had refused credit. Others say he was caught embezzling."

"What happened?"

"It must've been a small amount. After he was fired, he organized a *kompan* gang with four men from Fukuoka Prefecture. They worked the B-6 field for a couple of *kompan*s, then he bought Mr. Shoji's tofu business and piggery. No, I guess he wouldn't steal from his own petty cash."

We waited at the railroad tracks, which ran along the shore. When a locomotive came by, Aunt Kitano waved her parasol. The train stopped, and we ran and got on one of the flat cars.

It was scary riding at such speed, with the wind and soot blowing in our faces. We arrived at the mill in half an hour. An enormous smokestack towered over us. There was a deafening roar from the mill.

"Let's eat first," Aunt Kitano shouted. "There was a strike here in 1905. A *haole luna* beat up a Japanese worker and blinded one of his eyes. Fourteen hundred Japanese went on strike and came here to protest. The police fired on them and killed a striker and wounded two."

"What happened?"

"The manager fired the *luna* and gave us a small raise," she laughed. "The peasants in Japan used to rise up in protest, too. The Tokugawa government would make some concessions, then behead the leaders. The leaders knew each time they'd be beheaded."

We walked a couple of blocks and turned left. The ocean was on our right. It all came back, riding past these shops six months ago. It was the main street, bustling with pedestrians, cars, and hacks.

We stopped at a Japanese shop and had large bowls of saimin. I'd never tasted noodles so delicious. Then we ambled to the wharf. Yes, this is where I landed. A grand hotel sat across the wharf. People going to Wailuku often stayed overnight at the Pioneer Hotel, Isao had said.

Aunt Kitano pointed to the sampans anchored some distance from the wharf. "Most of the fishermen are Japanese."

"They look like the boats back home."

"The boat builders are Japanese. The whales come here in the fall to bear their young."

We sat under a banyan tree next to the courthouse.

"You see the buildings at the foot of that mountain? The white ones among the trees?" she asked.

"Yes."

"That's Pepelau Vocational High School. That's where Kisata is boarding."

"*Ah, so.*"

Kisata visited every couple of months. He'd bring several of his Japanese classmates. They were so hungry for rice, they'd walk down the gulch from the school, up a steep ridge, then down to the gulch above Kahana. Father Takao always killed a chicken, made *heka*, and bought sashimi. Nothing was too good for the scholars. Otherwise we ate tofu, miso soup, and *iriko*. After a few *sake*s, Father Takao would talk on and on about the value of education, the superiority of the Japanese spirit, and so on, as if he were reliving his student days.

"This is what I dreamed Hawaii would be like," I said as we walked back to the mill. "I wish we could live here."

"There're three company towns like Kahana on the outskirts, but for a Japanese to live in town, he has to be either a shopkeeper or fisherman."

Mother Haru was starting a fire at the outside stove when I got back.

"I'll do it," I said.

She handed me the tinder and mumbled as she walked off, "She feels no shame abandoning her children."

11 · The Theft Is Solved

In May the plantation began digging an irrigation tunnel through one of the mountains. The diggers lived at the site some five miles into the gulch above Kahana. Every Saturday one of the bachelor diggers rode into camp on horseback. He bought a week's ration for twenty, consisting of rice, pickles, dried or canned fish, and twenty-four dozen cakes of tofu. Father Takao, Chiyako, Kingo, and I worked feverishly to make twenty-eight dozen cakes by Saturday. "If this keeps up, we'll be returning to Japan soon," Father Takao said. Maybe because she was so busy or because the 25 cents wasn't disappearing, we'd go through weeks without Mother Haru's accusations.

In June Kisata quit Pepelau High School. He needed two more years to graduate, but he said he'd learned enough and wanted to find a job in Honolulu. Father Takao gave him money for boat fare and a week's expenses. He had worked only three years, then boarded at Pepelau High for three years. Now he was free.

Azumi was sent next to the school, but he quit after a month, and the plantation gave him back his old job of steam plow operator. In late September he caught a bad cold and stayed in bed. The *haole luna* came with a whip and chased him out of his room. He collapsed in the fields, and they carried him to our barracks. Father Takao made room for him in their cramped space, and Mother Haru fed him lots of *aburage* after burning off the oil. She boiled spinach, which grew like weeds in the backyard, and sprinkled it with sesame seeds. We fed him lots of tofu, rice, miso soup with seaweed, and the best portions of the occasional mackerel, pork, or chicken. He ran a high fever for over a week.

When he finally recovered, he walked like an old man. "I'm leaving. I can't stay here. They'll kill me if I stay."

"Wait till you regain your strength," Mother Haru said.

"I have to leave now! They'll kill me if I don't leave now!"

Father Takao gave him some money and Kisata's address in Honolulu. Isao got Azumi's belongings from the single men's housing, and I made him a lunch of two rice balls wrapped in seaweed with pickled plums in the center. The rest of the family woke up to say goodbye, and he went out into the darkness as if he were going off to work.

Father Takao was so unfair to Isao. He asked so much of Isao and so little of Kisata and Azumi. Isao had inherited all the disadvantages but none of the advantages of a number one son.

The accusations became a weekly thing about the time the tunnel was finished.

"No matter how much you steal, you won't be able to get it out. I'm checking the store," Mother Haru fumed.

"You're only tiring yourself."

"I hope Mrs. Kitano isn't teaching you to shirk your duties like she did."

"She's my Hawaiian mother," I said.

"She thinks she's great because she's the only midwife in camp. She charges way too much. The plantation hospital does it for free."

"She pays her own way."

I wasn't going to let Mother Haru have the last word. Poverty was new to her. Her parents had owned three large, white warehouses full of forfeited goods. She and her sister took lessons in music, poetry, singing, dancing, and flower arrangement—none of which we from peasant families could afford.

"She'll have to die here." Mother Haru trudged back into the barracks.

It always saddened me when I thought of Aunt Kitano lost in the vast, unfriendly ocean. We all have a little of the salmon in us. We all dream of returning to our native villages to die. It's a comfort to be buried among ancestors and to be cared for by grandchildren and great-grandchildren.

* * *

Mrs. Kitano was eighteen when her father died suddenly of a stroke. Three months before his death, carpenters from the neighboring village began renovating their farm house, and she fell in love with Mr. Ono, a carpenter's apprentice. A month after her father's death, she said she was going to visit his grave, and never returned. She eloped with Mr. Ono and sailed off to Hawaii as they'd planned before her father's death.

For an ordinary man, the mourning takes forty-nine days. His virtues and sins are weighed and his fate in the next world decided. The family is supposed to offer incense and prayers every seventh day for seven weeks and abstain from *sake,* meat, and any hair cutting. The mourners have to quarantine themselves in order not to defile others. What Mrs. Kitano did was unforgivable. Takao, then sixteen and head of the household, called a family council. Everybody agreed that her name should be erased from the family register as if she'd never existed.

Takao hated farming. He leased all eight acres and went to work as a clerk at the local police station. Unable to support his mother and siblings on his wages and the rent he collected, he kept selling off pieces of his land till he had only four acres left. When he proposed selling those, his uncles objected. The land had been in the family for eight generations. The family also owned the trees on one side of the 300-foot Mt. Konomi at the edge of the village. For 200 years each number one son had been headman of the village.

Takao promised he'd succeed in his *geta* store and buy back the land. He loved working with wood, and he'd make quality clogs from blocks of paulownia. He married Haru, who was a year older, and received a handsome dowry. He sold the rest of the farm and opened a store in Hakata and prospered. People loved the workmanship of his clogs and how they resonated on the cobblestones. Isao was born in 1894, Kisata in 1896, and Azumi in 1898. By then cheaper machine-made clogs of assembled parts destroyed his business. But Takao kept borrowing from his father-in-law. In 1901 Aya was born.

Six months later there was a big commotion in the village next to Omaru. Setsuko Ono, robust and very much in existence, returned with her husband and two sons. After thirteen years Mr. Ono had fulfilled every immigrant's dream of "returning to his native village bedecked in brocade." He had 2,000 yen ($1,000) in cash! They'd come back to farm out their sons to relatives so that they could grow up Japanese. Mr. Ono would pay generously for their keep, of course.

Takao rushed down from Hakata to greet his sister and brother-in-law. He had no intention of restoring her name to the family register.

"How did you manage to save so much money?" he asked.

"We both worked," Mr. Ono said. "Setsuko learned midwifery and I worked in the cane fields. Why don't you come to Hawaii with us? I'll loan you your boat fare."

"How much is that?"

"Eighty yen each. But you have to leave your children. They'll only get in your way."

Takao had to make up his mind quickly. The Onos were leaving in a couple of weeks. His younger brother, Masazo, a carpenter, agreed to look after their mother and sister.

Takao begged his father-in-law to look after his three sons. "I'll be back in five years."

Mr. Taniguchi, already in his sixties, said, "We'll look after them even if it means scratching on a rock with our fingernails."

※　※　※

In November I vomited outside the tofu shed. *Exhaustion has finally caught up with me,* I thought.

Then I noticed Chiyako wasn't yanking away her bowl of rice or shadowing me. She picked on Kingo instead, punching him and yelling at him in bursts of pidgin English.

"Stop bullying him," I said when the others did nothing.

Mother Haru had changed too, looking off when our eyes met. Did pregnancy give me so much status?

Then one night at supper, Father Takao had his two dispensers of *sake* and mumbled to himself, "Hmmm . . . Sawa is one cut above Isao."

What is he saying? How awful! Pretend you didn't hear! Nobody said anything for the rest of supper. Poor Isao ate and ran. *I don't want a compliment at the expense of my master!* I wanted to say.

"I'll do the dishes tonight, elder sister," Chiyako said.

"Let's do it together. It's faster."

"No, you need the rest. Kingo will help me. Come, Kingo!" Then she let fly another staccato jumble of words.

It's a miracle, I thought. *Pregnancy is a miracle.* "The womb is a borrowed thing," the farmers used to repeat the old samurai saying. But it worked both ways. As soon as you were carrying a child, especially a male child to carry on the paternal line, you became a hallowed vessel.

Two more weeks went by without Mother Haru's accusations. Had she been misplacing the money? *Am I imagining it or is she really avoiding me?* She hadn't asked me to comb her hair or massage her shoulders in four weeks. She must've found all the missing money.

"Mother hasn't accused me in over a month," I said when Aunt Kitano asked me. "I didn't realize pregnancy gave one so much status."

"She's probably realized she's been miscounting," she said.

"It feels so strange. I miss it suddenly. No, that's not true!" I caught my laughter in my palm. "But it gets to be a habit after a year!"

I finished the ironing and turned in at ten o'clock one night and found Isao awake.

"You're up late," I said as I lay beside him in the dark.

I had not brought up the subject since he ran away, but I couldn't help telling him, "You know, Mother hasn't accused me of stealing for a whole month! Since I got pregnant."

"Oh," he said sleepily, "Kingo's been taking it."

"What?"

"Mother caught him."

"When?!" I sprang up.

"I don't know." He turned away.

"Who told you?"

"Mother."

"When?"

"Couple of weeks ago."

"Last week?"

"Couple of weeks."

"Week before last?"

"Several weeks ago, I don't know."

"Several weeks ago, and you didn't tell me?!"

"I was waiting for the right moment."

"The right moment! You knew how miserable I was! Did she tell you to tell me?"

"No."

"What did she say?!"

"Just that Kingo had been taking it. He's only a child. He must've thought the money belonged to everybody."

"Did she say that?!"

"Something like that."

"What was he doing with the money?!"

"Buying chocolate candies."

"Where?!"

"The plantation store. Kuni Store."

"He kept on stealing, knowing I was being accused!"

"He's only a child."

"He's nine!"

"Shhh . . . they'll hear you."

"Let them! I couldn't even write home! It was too shameful! A whole year!"

"Shut up!"

"If it wasn't for Aunt Kitano, I'd have killed myself! Nobody else believed me, not even you!"

"Shhh . . . they'll hear you."

The curtain offered less privacy than a shoji screen. Now was the time to create a scene, make them cringe, pay them back—Mother Haru and her moneylender's mind; her spy Chiyako, "worse than a thousand devils"; the little thief, Kingo; my own husband who doubted me; and Father Takao in his *sake* heaven. Only Aunt Kitano had believed me. And baby Masako.

But I could no more make a scene than fly. I lay back. Tears rolled down my temples. I'm on the sandy bottom of a warm tropical ocean, wave after wave lapping gently over me, washing away the pain, the bone-tiredness.

12 · Kazue

Aunt Kitano asked after New Year's day, "There's been no more money disappearing?"

"Well . . ." I dumped her swill into one of our cans. I wasn't going to tell her unless she asked. "Kingo had been taking it."

"That little thief!"

"He's only nine. He must've thought the money belonged to everybody."

"Nonsense! Once or twice is excusable! But he did it for a whole year, week after week, knowing you were being blamed! He never stole before! He began after you came, knowing you'd be blamed! That takes the nerve of a professional thief!"

I still could not imagine his stealing. He looked so skinny in his short pants.

"He must've really craved chocolates," I said.

"He could've chewed cane like the rest of the children."

"Well, I think they all feel bad. They're treating me extra nice."

"Did Haru tell you about it?"

"No, my husband did."

"She never will either! She'll ignore it and pretend it never happened. You know, all the things they said about Takao are probably true. He must've been fired for stealing."

"You're being too harsh."

She laughed. "No, there's some real bumps on our family line."

"I don't know what I would've done without you. I had nobody to talk to. Thank you very much."

I even need her to get angry for me, I thought as I pushed off.

I wrote a long letter home. For a whole year, I had scribbled short notes. "Everything is fine. Please don't worry. I'm so busy. I'll write later." "Are you all right? What's the matter?" Mother kept asking. Now I wrote that a grandchild was due in July and that I missed the rice planting, the harvest, and the moon viewing, but Hawaii had so many marvelous things. The flowers were so beautiful and fragrant. Kahana sat 500 feet above the sea, and the sky turned into an orange-red hibiscus at sunset. The mountains had so much rain, the peaks looked moss covered. And the fruits were of all shapes and tastes: papaya, mango, passion fruit, soursop, avocado, banana, coconut. I'd eaten one of each since they said on the *Tenyo Maru* that you lived seventy-five days longer for every new thing you ate. The heat was intense, but so were the colors, and cockroaches grew to enormous sizes. And the water in Kahana was pure rainwater from the intake in the mountains. I'd never tasted water so cold and delicious. I got up every morning at three to make tofu. The air was so cool and fresh, the day's dust hadn't risen yet, and my thoughts were crystal clear. It was exhilarating to get a jump on the rest of the world. The first light was so soft and radiant, I'd keep thinking of the first dawn, *Amaterasu Omikami,* emerging from the rock cave of Heaven.

I wanted to tell them about how Aunt Kitano practically saved my life. But how could I praise her without bad-mouthing Mother Haru and the others? Praising one meant also blaming another. It was best not to talk about it—not in any detail, anyway.

Soon afterward Father Takao moved the family to quarters that had been vacated, in a barracks farther up the road. Families were always moving from one barracks to another.

"Let's stay here," I said to Isao.

He looked puzzled.

"Instead of moving with them, let's live here. Other couples have their own quarters."

"I don't think Father will approve."

"Shall I ask him?"

He shrugged.

"We'll need more space when the baby comes. We're nearer the pigpens, so feeding the pigs will be easier. Mother is stronger now, and she can do the chores with Chiyako's help. I'll still be doing the tofu, pigs, laundry, and ironing. Will you ask them?"

I finally quit nagging him. What if he ran away again? But why was he so afraid of displeasing his parents? Why did they treat him so shabbily? Kingo was still their golden prince. His thievery had just been a prank. They must've made up their minds that they would depend on Kingo in their old age. He was their true number one son.

I was careful not to press my belly against the handle of the cart. One morning I thought my water bag broke when I was collecting pig swill. It hadn't, but I was bleeding. I went back to the house, and Aunt Kitano arrived.

"Wait for the cramps," she said.

The contractions began at dusk, and then my water broke.

"Feels uncomfortable."

"That'll speed up the contractions," came Aunt Kitano's voice.

They came in waves, twisting and squishing my insides. "It hurts! It hurts!"

"There, that wasn't so bad, was it?" she asked, wiping my forehead with a damp rag. "You're doing well. It won't get any worse."

But suddenly it started again! "It hurts! It hurts!" Nobody had told me about the pain!

Hours crawled by. I doubled over and clenched my teeth to ride out the pain.

"Shouldn't we take her to the hospital?" Mother Haru's voice was far away.

"No, she'll be all right." Aunt Kitano, too, seemed smaller. "Can you push a little more?"

I've floated up and am looking down at myself and the others. It's happening again, the moment before I black out.

"Push! Push! Push, Sawa-chan!" Aunt Kitano's deep voice resonates about the room.

Push-push-push, it's all I have left; then I feel my guts being pulled out. Suddenly a swoosh of air and I'm back in my body and a baby cries.

"It's a girl," Aunt Kitano said. She cleaned her and handed me the pink blob.

The others came in from beyond the curtain.

"She's cute for a newborn," Father Takao said.

"She already needs a haircut," Mother Haru said.

Isao named her Kazue. I stayed in bed for two weeks. Kazue never stopped crying. She couldn't digest my milk. Even miso soup and cow's milk gave her diarrhea. I strapped her to my back when I went to sell tofu. Masako baby-sat when I did the laundry or went to get pig grass. I took her to the Kahana dispensary. Dr. Hall, who was there from noon to one o'clock every weekday, couldn't find anything wrong.

"Why is she so irritable?" I asked Shizuko-san, the nurse's aide.

"The doctor can't find anything wrong with her," she said.

Three months later Kazue died of pneumonia. She'd been sick from the moment she was born. We buried her in the Jodo Buddhist graveyard, in a clearing in the sandy *kiawe* grove near Kaanapali landing.

* * *

America entered the Great War in the spring. In June there was a commotion in camp. All the young men, nisei and issei, went to Pepelau to register for the draft, but nobody got called. The war tripled the prices of rice, soy beans, and other foodstuff while plantation pay remained the same. It cut into our tofu profit.

"Why don't you work in the fields? It's so much easier," the other brides kept saying. I asked Isao if we could form our own *kompan* like the other couples when his present one expired.

"If they don't need you at home," he said.

I spoke to Father Takao and Mother Haru one night after supper. "I'll be making $13 a month. That's more than half of our tofu profit. I'll work the first twenty days for the bonus, then stay home to help with the chores . . ."

Father Takao sighed and looked at Mother Haru.

"Let's see, twenty working days will leave seven or eight days at the end of the month." Mother Haru counted, flicking her fingers. "I think we can manage."

We got a four-acre *kompan*. The plantation supplied the seedlings, fertilizer, and water, and we did the planting, irrigation, and weeding. When the cane was harvested in two years, they paid us so much per ton as stipulated in the contract, minus the cost of fertilizer, any weeding done by others, and our daily wages of 77 cents for Isao and 57 cents for me.

On the first day I kept losing my hat.

"Here, I'll fix that," Isao said, and attached a chin strap.

"Why are we wearing all these heavy clothes? It's so hot!"

"Wait till the cane shoots up. The leaves are like saw blades," he said.

Isao did all the hard work, like shoring up the banks of the furrows or making *pani* bundles out of cane leaves to block and divert the water's course. I took a nap after lunch, and he let me sleep as long as I wanted. He was a different person away from his parents. Irrigating was fun, but hoe *hana* or weeding was back breaking. The weeds kept coming back, choking off the young cane.

I still helped with dinner and did the ironing, but now I bathed early. I soaked in the clean water and talked story with the other working wives. Sundays I did the sewing and other light work. Isao went to church in the mornings, then went back for the Methodist young men's club in the afternoons. *It'd be so nice to escape like him,* I kept thinking, but he needed to get away from Mother Haru's nagging.

"What do you do all afternoon?" I asked.

"We talk."

"What about?"

"The war, books, everything."

July fourth was an extra-big celebration. The plantation put on a horse race on the dirt road in the cane fields. August thirty-first was the emperor's birthday, and the plantation gave us another holiday without pay. I helped Mother Haru and Chiyako with the festival dishes, and Reverend Morimoto and the Methodist club put on a play for the whole camp. Isao wrote and directed it and cast his friends from the club. It was about a feudal lord in Kyushu who was persecuted and killed by the Tokugawa government for having become a Christian.

"It's a true story," he said.

"Where did you learn about him?" I said.

"The reverend's books," he said.

The next month I found I was pregnant.

I begged Father Takao to increase our allowance to $5.

13 · Toshio

The third New Year came and went. And we got days off on July fourth and August thirty-first. Isao wrote another play, but it wasn't as exciting as the last one. The novelty was gone.

In early November the *haole* boss came charging up on his horse. "War *pau*. War *pau*; bang-bang, all *pau*."

"Oh, *goodo, goodo,*" Isao nodded.

The *haole*s and *luna*s drove around camp tooting their horns. *Maybe now the prices will stabilize,* I thought.

I quit three months before term. I didn't want to be so rundown this time. The weeds were no problem once the cane grew tall, but now the irrigation was exhausting. We shucked the old leaves clogging the furrows. We deepened the channels on the furrow banks so that the water would run down into the furrows below. We pushed our way through the thick growth, shielding our faces from the saw-toothed leaves. It was so hot and suffocating, sweat drenched our thick shirts and pants.

Isao said he could work the fields by himself for the remaining eight months. Within a month the irrigating would be cut to every thirty days instead of the present fifteen.

A couple of months later a flu epidemic hit Kahana. Everybody wore white surgical masks. *It's just another flu season,* I thought, when suddenly old Mr. Goto died, then Mr. Matsuda. Dr. Hall and Shizuko-san came to the dispensary and said that it was a new strain of Spanish flu and that people on the mainland were dying from it. Everybody avoided contact with the stricken except Reverend Morimoto. Day and night he called on the sick of his congregation, bringing them food, doing their chores, and sharing Bible lessons and prayers with them. He must've exhausted himself. He died instantly when he was stricken.

It stunned the whole camp. He was only forty-one!

It hit Isao very hard. He walked about in a daze.

"You were really fond of him," I said.

He nodded and turned away to hide the tears.

"Why did you become a Christian?" I had asked when I'd first arrived. "It was the only place with social life on Sundays. The Buddhists didn't even have a temple," he'd said. Maybe that was the initial reason, but what kept him going back was Reverend Morimoto. He had come to Hawaii as a contract laborer in 1894 and became a Christian in 1899. He was so energetic, the young men flocked to his church. He also had a beautiful hand, and people went to him for their letters. He didn't drink or put up a big face. People trusted him more. He was the true headman of the village.

The plantation put Madame Morimoto on its payroll so that she could support her three children and continue her nursery for working mothers. She also continued her late husband's social work. *Being nisei and fluent in English, she won't have much trouble,* I thought. It'd be unthinkable if it had happened to one of us.

The Methodist young men's club still met every other Sunday, but Isao's old enthusiasm was gone. The membership began to dwindle from its original thirty members. The young men were leaving for Pepelau and Honolulu.

Aunt Kitano said I should go to the plantation hospital since I'd had such a hard time with Kazue. But it was another difficult birth. My hips were too narrow, Dr. Hall said. Isao named the boy Toshio, using the characters for "combatant."

I prayed he'd be able to digest my milk. He didn't cry as much as Kazue, but his stool worried me. It wasn't diarrhea, but it wasn't solid. Then, after a month of coaxing, he produced his first precious nuggets!

I strapped him to my back wherever I went. "*Oppa, oppa,*" I said, bouncing him when he cried. When I let him down, he'd cry to get back on.

"Let him cry; you're spoiling him," Isao kept saying.

Then it happened! Instead of crying, he said, "Oba, oba," meaning "*oppa.*"

"He spoke his first word today!" I announced to the family. He wasn't going to be retarded! It was bad enough worrying about kleptomania and chronic fatigue in the family tree.

* * *

In January 1920 the Filipino and Japanese plantation workers on Oahu went on strike, asking for a raise from 77 cents a day to $1.25 for men, and from 57 cents to 93 cents for women. The price of rice, miso, and soy beans had quadrupled since 1915.

"I don't think it'll spread," Father Takao said at supper. "The same thing happened in 1909. Only Oahu went on strike, but we all got raises afterward."

A month later, Father Takao got a letter from his younger brother, Masazo, saying his mother was gravely ill. In another month, Grandmother Oyama was dead.

"Well, *I* never got to see *my* parents either," Mother Haru said. "If we don't go back soon, they'll call you 'Urashima Taro.' You shouldn't have let Kisata and Azumi go. I begged you not to. It's not enough with just Isao working. If the strike spreads to Maui, we'll have to feed seven mouths on just tofu and pigs."

"Let's wait for Isao's *kompan* dollar," Father Takao said. "We'll be just in time for Aya's graduation." He'd been sending money for Aya's room, board, and tuition at Munakata Normal School.

The next month the plantation harvested our field. The *kompan* dollar came to $300.

The strike ended July first, and a couple months later all the workers in Kahana got a 50 percent raise.

Soon after New Year's day Father Takao began selling off the forty-nine pigs. The newborn piglets were $5 each, those five months old $25.35, the sows $100. He went about the camp asking for bids on his tofu equipment. He bought boat tickets for five for early March.

In February Toshio and Isao were hospitalized with diphtheria. Mr. Sakamoto and other callers brought Toshio several bags of Hershey's chocolates. There were so many, I unwrapped a bar and ate it. I'd never tasted anything so creamy and delicious! No wonder Kingo got addicted to them!

"Shall I ask your father to leave you some money?" Mr. Sakamoto asked Isao.

"Oh, I'm sure he will," Isao said.

"I don't think so. I know him better than you do," Mr. Sakamoto said. He was Father Takao's age.

"Don't worry. I'm sure he will," Isao said.

My stomach ached. It had never occurred to me that Father Takao wouldn't leave us some money. Even if he took all of our *kompan* dollar, he wouldn't leave us broke. I'd been so happy, thinking we'd finally be on our own. Now I couldn't stop worrying.

"Why don't we ask Mr. Sakamoto to ask for us?" I suggested.

"Don't worry. Father won't leave us penniless," he said.

When Isao and Toshio came home, I secreted the Hershey's bars in my wicker basket. One day I couldn't find the bags of chocolates! *Kingo!* I thought, blood pulsing at my temples.

At supper I said, my voice quavering, "What's happened to Toshio's candies? I had them in my wicker basket. They're gone."

"Oh, I took them. I need them as gifts," Father Takao said.

"All of them?" I was near tears.

"I haven't bought any gifts. I don't have the money for gifts. These would be just the thing," he said.

Then he bought seven cases of illegal beer on credit from Mr. Tani in Pepelau for his farewell party.

"You must talk to him!" I said to Isao. "He's planning a big party for himself and leaving us all the bills! He'll leave us nothing to live on!"

"Don't worry, he'll give us something," Isao said.

Every day I asked him, "Did you ask him?"

"No."

"You must ask him today!"

"You don't think much of him, do you?"

"I just go by what I see. You have to ask him!"

He'd been scolded so much he was afraid to ask them for anything.

"Now's your chance," I said when Father Takao was alone at the outside stove.

"Father, we don't have any money to live on after you leave," Isao said.

"I came here penniless, but I've made a success of myself. You can do the same!" he barked.

"Please, Father! I came here to raise the colors of your house!" I trembled, tears streaming. "I worked without complaining! But we need something to live on for the next month! It's not only us! There's Toshio, and I'm expecting another child! We need something to live on! We gave everything to you!"

"Please . . . you're still young. I'll be forty-eight soon. I have three children of school age. I have all the debts in Japan I have to repay. The boat fare alone costs over $200. We'll need winter clothes in Japan. Then I need money to start some kind of business. I need every penny." A tear rolled down his cheek. "I can't ask for more filial children. I'll send for you as soon as I'm successful. And when you come, you need not bring any gifts; you can come with just the clothes on your backs."

I was no worrywart! Everything I had worried about came true!

The party was set for Sunday, and everybody was invited. A tarp was spread overhead between two barracks, and Aunt Kitano and the other women came to help. Every guest brought a *sembetsu*, a parting gift of money, ranging from $1 to $10 in a white envelope. I recorded the name and amount of each gift. It came to $400. Isao and I would have to repay the same amount to each donor some day. The bills on the food came to $600!

The villagers toasted Father Takao and thanked him for the letters he'd written and the favors he'd done them. You're returning home a success, they said.

The following morning he had the Mikami taxi come up from Pepelau.

"I'll leave you with the taxi bill," he said to Isao as he got into the cab.

I was so angry and depressed that I wept. I turned once more to Aunt Kitano.

"He even took all of Toshio's candies."

Aunt Kitano, now fifty, puffed her long pipe with its tiny metal bowl and tapped the ashes into the ash tray made from a tin can. It fit into the homemade wooden tobacco box.

"They call people like him 'uchi benkei,' 'kage benkei,' 'uchi ni kaereba tenka sama' . . ." She dug up all the sayings—there were so many of them—describing husbands who were timid in public but bossy at home. ". . . He'd sacrifice his children just to put up a big face," she said.

"You know, I even feel sorry for Mother," I said.

"He'll get his *bachi*. He has nobody to leech onto in Japan. Returning home a success—it's a laugh. He's a failure. He loses the family farm, he comes here to make money to buy it back, he stays for nineteen years and lets his mother die in poverty. He spends lavishly, pretending he's wealthy. He's not fooling anybody. What can he do in Japan? Buy back the farm? Open another *geta* store? Prices must've quintupled. I hate to say this of a younger brother, but you're lucky to be rid of him. He can see only what's owed him, never what he owes."

PART III * *1921–1929*

14 · Joji

Isao went to his best friend, Kawai Ichiro, and borrowed $10. In 1920 the plantation had promoted Ichiro to *luna* of the steam plow gang. Any Japanese five feet seven inches or taller had a good chance of being appointed straw boss of a Japanese gang. At twenty-six he was the youngest *luna*. He invited Isao to join his gang.

Two steam plow engines at opposite ends of the field pulled a harrow back and forth by means of a cable, Isao explained. The men had to move the harrow to its next position, then pull the braided iron cable from the other steam plow and hook it to the harrow. Isao was the smallest of the gang, and he was assigned to refuel and oil the machines. "I'm the engineer," he said.

Father Takao wrote from Kokura. They had hoped to attend Aya's graduation from Munakata Normal School. But the ceremony was already over when they arrived. Aya ran toward the station, and mother and daughter embraced and wept. "We're staying at Mr. Taniguchi's," Father Takao said. *Poor Uncle Taniguchi,* I thought. *He must be slouching even more.*

The plantation garnisheed half of Isao's pay to pay for the bills Father Takao had run up at the plantation store.

"We can't live on $10 a month. We go $10 into debt every month even while eating tofu and *iriko,*" I said.

Isao borrowed $10 from Ichiro again, and the next month I asked Aunt Kitano for $10.

"We have to do something. Maybe we should start a *tanomoshi,*" I said.

"Yes, let's do it," Isao said.

We decided on a $100 *tanomoshi*.

"So you'll start organizing it tomorrow?" I asked.

"No, you do it."

"But whoever heard of a woman organizing a *tanomoshi?!*"

"It was your idea. You do it."

"But it's for both of us!"

"You do it!" he yelled. "I hate handling money!"

"Who doesn't?!"

"It was your idea. You do it!"

"Aren't you afraid people will laugh?

"Shut up!"

I'd learned not to press him. After *"Yakamashii!"* his backhand might flash out.

I asked Aunt Kitano first. "We're starting a $100 *tanomoshi* with ten people. Could you please join?"

"Of course," she said.

Then I asked Mrs. Kuni, the widow. Seven to go, but now I had to speak to the men. I felt queasy, like when I first hawked tofu. I called on the people from Fukuoka Prefecture. They were the closest thing to an extended family. I *oppa*ed Toshio and called on the families after supper. Mr. Kawai, Mr. Kanda, Mr. Shiotsugu, Mr. Aoki, Mr. Antoku, and the others seemed surprised to see me, but they joined without hesitation.

The first meeting was called on the night of the next payday. Aunt Kitano, Mrs. Kuni, and the seven men each brought $10. I served tea and rice crackers, and Isao acted as host and moderator. We took the first $100. The $100 at the next meeting was up for bids, and the highest bid was divided among the eight unpaid participants. We would meet once a month until the tenth member got the last $100. Isao came alive at these meetings. He enjoyed being moderator and host. He kept the conversation flowing, and he could speak on practically any subject, but he always drew out the others to speak and participate. They left happy.

A few months later, Mr. Murai of Pepelau came through Kahana selling a new type of sewing machine made by the Singer Company. If he could get ten orders, he'd have somebody come and teach smocking to the buyers. "We need one more!" "Sawa-san, you have to be the tenth!" the other wives said. I kept refusing. Where would we get $50? Besides, we'd just bought a kerosene stove on credit. The plantation now gave us ten gallons of kerosene a month instead of firewood. But I kept thinking that if I learned Western-style sewing, I could sew work pants and shirts and make back $50 in no time.

"Go ahead," Isao said.

"I'll ask Mr. Murai if I can put $10 down and pay him $10 a month. The lessons will last two months, so we'll have most of it paid up by then."

Mr. Murai put the ten machines in an empty barracks he rented from the plantation, and he had Mr. Terada from Pepelau teach us for two hours every Wednesday. The others chatted and laughed through their lessons, but I hardly looked up. I was spending $50 we could ill afford. Then I had to keep hushing Toshio. Another child was kicking in my belly.

"You have a knack for sewing," Mr. Terada said.

"Is there anything else?" I was always the first to finish.

After five months, Mr. Murai gave each of us a certificate.

"I graduated number one. Everybody said I was the best," I said to Isao.

In July I had a boy at the plantation hospital in Pepelau. I was in labor for sixteen hours. Dr. Hall said I shouldn't have any more children because my hips were too narrow. Isao named him Joji, using the characters for "contributor."

He was such a healthy, mellow child. His stool was first-rate, and he rarely cried or woke me up in the middle of the night, but now Toshio began to *amaeru,* acting up and begging to be coddled. Once while nursing Joji, I heard Toshio shrieking like a piglet being castrated. I rushed outside. Isao was holding him upside down by the ankle, threatening to drop him!

I grabbed Toshio. "What are you doing?!"

"You're only spoiling him!"

Maybe I did spoil him. Life had been so miserable in those days. He'd been my only joy. But now at the church potlucks and picnics, he picked on Hiroshi Miyake, who was six months younger. He'd use Hiroshi as a horse and yank his hair, yelling, "Giddyap! Giddyap!" I'd say, "You should let Hiroshi-san ride you now," but as soon as I looked away he'd be whipping and kicking his "horse" again.

"Children will be children," Mrs. Miyake would laugh mirthlessly, and she'd always sit the farthest from us. But it didn't stop Toshio.

One day Isao slapped him on the side of the head. "Didn't I tell you to leave Hiroshi-san alone!"

Toshio screamed.

"You hit him like he's an adult!" I hugged Toshio. With all his faults, Father Takao never once raised his voice or hit anybody. I couldn't imagine where Isao got his short temper.

My mother wrote from Ikeura. No news had been good news. Now Father was dead. "He must've lost his will to live. He lay down one day and refused to get up. The doctors could find nothing wrong . . ."

"You're his substitute," I murmured to Joji.

I felt so tired. I'd have seen my father again if I'd returned in five years.

"I feel I'm going to die," I told Aunt Kitano.

"Don't be silly," she said. "You're only . . . what . . . twenty-five."

"Twenty-four by Japanese age. But everything keeps rushing on top of me. I have to lie down to keep from blacking out."

"It's just depression; you'll get over it. It's a Japanese disease," she laughed.

"Why?"

"I don't know. They pile too much on us, and we tend to *gaman* too much."

I showed her Father Takao's letter from Tokyo. They'd stayed six months at Uncle Taniguchi's. Then Father Takao's younger brother, Saburo Yamada, the adopted husband, now the president of Tokyo Technical College, got him a contract with the Ajinomoto Company in Tokyo, making paper wrappers for their monosodium glutamate. "We're so busy, even Masako is helping. We've finally hit it!" he wrote. "We wanted Aya to come with us, but she's under contract to teach for two years in Munakata County."

"I hope he succeeds," Aunt Kitano said.

Mr. Naito drove up to Kahana once a week to solicit orders for the Tabata Dry Goods Store in Pepelau. He would stop for tea and talk story even when there was no order.

One evening, after listening to Isao, he said, "Why don't you quit the plantation and become a fisherman? My father raised the eight of us as a fisherman. He couldn't have done so working on the plantation."

"I think I'll become a fisherman," Isao said two weeks later. He'd skipped church and gone to Pepelau on Sunday.

"But you don't know anything about fishing," I said.

"Mr. Nishida says he'll hire me. He needs a helper."

"But you've got a good job now. What will you say to Ichiro-san?"

"He's my best friend. He'll understand."

I was not entirely against it. Our *tanomoshi* was finally finished, but we were still broke. Nobody got rich working in the fields. The Kandas succeeded because the family ran the bakery and restaurant for the single men. The plantation even collected for them, withholding what was owed them from each client's pay. The Kandas had come from the same Munakata County as the Oyamas, and the Kanda parents had returned to their native village in glory. Now the number one son, Hideo, who was Isao's age, ran the bakery-restaurant. They were the only Japanese in Kahana to own land.

"Another thing," Isao said. "If we move to Pepelau, we can run away from the obligations Father incurred."

"Yes, it'll be nice to run away from all the *kosai*," I laughed.

But we had to pay off the $40 we owed the plantation store. Isao went to Kanda Hideo and borrowed $100. Isao quit the plantation in December and went to work for Mr. Nishida.

We moved to a building behind Back Street one block from the ocean. The Koga Dry Goods Store was at the corner of Back Street and Dickensen. Past Koga Store a dirt alley led to our large three-room wood frame house. A large *ohai* tree stood in front of the veranda. Past the alley on Back Street were the Oshiro Tailor Shop and the Ando Metal Shop.

A few weeks after we moved in, Mr. Aoki of Kahana, who'd given us his pig swill, asked if we could board his number one son while he waited for an opening at the Pepelau High School dormitories. He'd pay us $5 a month for his food. The Aokis were like extended family.

"Wouldn't people talk, having a bachelor in the house while you're at sea?" I asked.

"He's just finished grade school—he's a boy of fourteen!" Isao scoffed.

Toshio and Joji took up all my energies. *How am I going to care for another child?* I worried. But boarding Aoki Nobuo turned out to be easy. He ate breakfast with us, I made him a lunch of rice balls, and he walked up to Pepelau High School. He went directly to the Methodist language school afterward and returned at dusk to bathe and sup on fish and rice, which we had plenty of. Then he studied in the kitchen till late at night.

I put down the futon for him in the parlor and put a coil of mosquito punk in Isao's tobacco box next to his pillow. He didn't have mosquito netting, but the punk would last half the night if he lit it before going to bed.

He was no trouble, but I felt so tired. I'd wake up tired and would barely last the day. I had only Toshio and Joji to look after now, but I could hardly finish the simplest task. Had Joji's birth sapped my strength? Or was I afflicted with Mother Haru's chronic fatigue?

"I feel like I'm going to die," I said one night, lying beside Isao and cuddling Joji.

"Don't be silly."

"My strength isn't returning."

It was a relief of sorts when there was a vacancy and Aoki Nobuo moved up to the Pepelau school dormitory.

"I feel more rundown than when I bore Kazue," I told Isao.

"Come, I'll take you to see Dr. Hall."

"It'll cost $3."

"That's all right."

"I feel so tired and dizzy," I told Shizuko-san. Dr. Hall recommended complete rest. I should leave Toshio and Joji and go up to Kula Sanitarium, which was a tuberculosis sanitarium built by the federal government on the slopes of Haleakala.

"We can't afford it," I said.

"The care there is free," Shizuko-san said. Dr. Hall arranged to have me admitted.

"There's no danger of catching tuberculosis?" I asked. Consumption ran in our family.

Dr. Hall laughed. "No."

We entrusted four-month-old Joji to a wet nurse, Mrs. Arisumi, in Honokawai. He bawled and wouldn't let go of me. Kawai Jiro and his wife would stay at our house rent free and feed, bathe, and clothe Toshio when Isao was out at sea. Jiro was Ichiro's younger brother and had belonged to the Kahana Methodist young men's club. He'd married a woman from Tokyo and now worked as a fishmonger. He'd buy fish from fishermen who weren't committed to fish markets and wheel his pushcart around Pepelau and the Mill, Kiawe, and Pump camps.

"I'm sorry to be such a burden," I said to Isao. I cuddled Toshio as we rode the Mikami taxi to Wailuku and up Haleakala.

"Don't be silly."

"The debt just keeps growing."

"Don't worry about the debt. Your health is more important."

"I hope the children will be all right."

Isao had to drag Toshio back to the taxi.

I felt so empty afterward. Joji was still a part of my flesh.

The next day I sat outside in the wan sunlight and watched a butterfly wafting from flower to flower. *How much longer does it have to live?* I thought. I kept rubbing the slight cleft at the tip of my nose. People with such clefts died young, the villagers said. Death and sadness were everywhere.

"I feel like I've climbed into Heaven," Teruko, another patient, said in a hushed voice.

"Can you imagine a place like this in Japan?" Mitsue whispered.

We felt like conspirators in the presence of awesome Haleakala. There were a dozen picture brides in the two nontubercular cottages. The other ten cottages housed the consumptives.

"We're so lucky. They're not even permitted to walk in the yard," Teruko said. "Very few consumptives who come up here ever go back down again."

Teruko had four children; Mitsue, five. They'd both worked in the cane fields till they'd literally collapsed. "I'm such a crybaby; I shouldn't *amaeru* so," I said to myself.

There was an autumn chill without the autumn colors. We wore layers of clothes and *haori* jackets or shawls and walked with unhurried grace. The garden felt summery with poincianas, red-skinned avocadoes, poinsettias, geraniums, red ginger, willows, and gardenia. Skylarks hovered overhead, trilling their birdsongs. Rainbows arced across the *makai* sky. San-O-sama's hillock was an anthill compared to Haleakala, which gave birth to the sun each morning. In the afternoons the fog would creep down the massive slope and shroud the bean-sized cattle, trees, and cacti.

"Rest, don't excite yourselves," Dr. Sherwood kept saying.

Milk was served with every meal. It gave us diarrhea.

"I don't see how you ladies are getting your calcium," Miss Kaya translated for Dr. Sherwood.

They served cheese, which stank of butter and crumbled in our mouths like clay. We had meat once a day—beef stew, meat loaf, hamburger, hot dogs, or pork. There was enough meat in one dish to flavor a dozen vegetable dishes! No wonder the *haoles* were so tall!

Isao came up in the Mikami taxi once every two weeks. He and Toshio would visit Joji in Honokawai, then backtrack to Pepelau and come east. Toshio would jump into my arms and refuse to let go. Joji was getting fat on Mrs. Arisumi's milk, Isao assured me.

We sat in the cool afternoon sun. Green pastures swept down from the sanitarium to the patchwork of cane fields in the flatlands. Farther *makai* was the town of Kahului and the blue ocean rising to the horizon. Beyond Kahului were the lush green peaks of the West Maui mountains.

"Pepelau is just beyond those mountains," Isao said.

"*Ah so.* So we're actually two mountains joined by Wailuku."

* * *

Toshio seemed so desperate on their next visit. He held me so tightly I could scarcely breathe. "What's the matter?" I tilted his face. His ribs and arms felt bony.

"He's lost some weight. Are you feeding him enough?"

"Yes, when I'm home."

"What about Jiro and his wife?"

"I give them $5 a month. That should be plenty."

"I understand she's very haughty and leads him around by the nose."

"She's a Tokyo girl, unlike other brides. And they're both heavy drinkers."

"Won't they get arrested?"

Isao shrugged. "Everybody does it."

"I'd feel better if somebody else looked after Toshio."

"There's nobody else."

The taxi cost $5. Isao was making $25, compared to the $20 on the plantation, but rent, medical care, water, and kerosene were no longer free. He talked of borrowing $500 from Tani Fish Market to buy his own sampan.

"*Soh, ne?*" I said, feeling strangely detached.

15 · Kiyoshi

It was on their fifth visit. Toshio jumped into my arms and bawled.

"What's the matter?"

"I've boarded him at the Buddhist girls' school in Wailuku," Isao said. "Mrs. Ando came to me when I got back from sea a week ago. She said Jiro and his wife drank a lot and did not feed Toshio. She'd seen him searching the garbage cans. She wanted to feed him, she said, but she didn't want to offend the Kawais."

"How awful! I told you he looked thinner. Weren't you aware of it? You must've seen how dirty he was. They probably never bathed him."

Soon after Mie-chan (Mrs. Ando) told Isao, he went looking for somewhere to board Toshio. Mr. Omori, his barber, boarded his twelve-year-old daughter at the Buddhist language school in Wailuku.

"Oh, I'm sure they'll take him. I'll ask my daughter, Sumiko, to look after him," Mr. Omori said. So Isao paid off Jiro and left Toshio in Wailuku.

"How do you like sleeping with Sumi-chan?" I asked.

"I hate it!"

"Do they feed you every day?"

He nodded.

"But you don't like it?"

He shook his head vigorously.

"They must tease him," Isao laughed.

"It's a good thing Mie-chan told you. Imagine spending days and nights with drunken strangers! I never cared for Jiro. He has bad posture. Even his face looks twisted. How can his elder brother be so honorable and he so good-for-nothing?"

Toshio bawled and wouldn't let go when it was time to leave.

Two months later Dr. Sherwood said I could go home. I had regained ten pounds and was back at ninety-five pounds.

"Sank you, sank you." I bowed and bowed. How could I ever repay him?

Isao and Toshio came for me in Mr. Mikami's taxi. Riding down from Kula, I felt I'd been given a new life and was being returned to the wondrous earth. I'd missed suckling Joji. How was he?

We stopped at the Buddhist language school in Wailuku.

"Come," I said, taking Toshio's hand.

Suddenly he burst out crying, screaming and kicking and hitting my forearm.

It hurt so much my eyes watered. "What's the matter with you? We're only going in to thank them!"

He whimpered and pressed himself into the corner.

"All right, you wait here."

Isao and I went in to thank the priest.

At Honokawai I had another shock. Joji bawled and wouldn't let go of his wet nurse. I cooed and bounced him and offered him my breast, but he kept reaching for Mrs. Arisumi and screaming like a piglet. *How awful!* I thought. *Your own flesh and blood can forget you in four months!*

"We've come just in time," Isao said. "He doesn't even know his real mother."

But my biggest shock was when I got home. There were bills amounting to over $300 charged in Isao's name.

"I didn't want to tell you till we got home," Isao said.

"Who's this Nakamura? There's a Nakamura Store in Pepelau?"

"He's a bootlegger. He makes beer."

"They spent this much in four months? He spends all this money while starving Toshio? I can't believe it!"

"Don't worry, Ichiro will repay me."

"What's wrong with his younger brother?"

"It's his wife. She thinks she's too good for Hawaii."

"Where is he now?'

"They both ran away to Honolulu."

"He must not have been working the months he was here. How can Ichiro-san be so honorable and he so crooked?"

I learned the next week that Jiro had bought smaller amounts of beer and groceries in other people's names. As a fishmonger, he had to compete with the fish markets, which had automobiles and fresher fish.

"Have you spoken to Ichiro-san yet?" I kept asking.

"How can I? I've been at sea all week!"

"You have to talk to him! He might not even know!"

"Don't worry, he'll pay."

"That's what you said about Father."

"He'll pay, I'm telling you!"

"But there're other people he has to repay too. Ours is the largest so ours should be first."

When I asked him several days later, he said, "I heard he took out a *tanomoshi*. He'll probably pay me with that."

"Did he ask you to join the *tanomoshi?*"

"No."

"Isn't that strange? You're his best friend. You always ask your friends first."

"He must realize it's inconvenient for me, living in Pepelau."

"But if it's to pay you back, he should ask you. Just out of courtesy. Have you talked to him?"

"No."

"Why not?"

"I haven't had the chance!"

"Why don't you go to Kahana to talk to him?"

"I'll talk to him when I see him!"

"He might not even know!"

"He knows! I wrote him!"

"What did he say?"

"I haven't heard!"

"Why don't you write him again?"

"Once is enough! We're like brothers!"

"Well, Jiro was his real brother. Maybe he's like Jiro."

"Shut up!"

He had learned to drink while I was at Kula.

"I can't refuse when Nishida offers me," he said.

"Do you drink at sea?"

"Never! The sea can turn on you in a second."

But now he drank at home and got amorous when drunk. I hated the reek of beer. Once during our lovemaking Toshio got up and crawled about half-asleep while Isao stopped literally in midair.

A month went by without any word from Kawai Ichiro.

"We would have heard by now if he took out the *tanomoshi* to pay us. You should hire Mikami and go see him."

"He's working when I'm free, and I'm working when he's free!"

A month later I was pregnant and Mr. Shinagawa died. Birth and death always came in pairs. He was only thirty-six. He had picked at a sore in his nostril. It became infected, and he was dead in a week. It shocked everyone. It was so sudden and unexpected.

Being from Fukuoka, he had given us his pig swill. Isao arranged to take Sunday off for the funeral. I checked our ledger to see how much he had given for Father Takao's farewell gift. I put $10 in a white envelope. Poor Emi-chan; how was she going to support herself and her children? She seemed too frail to work in the fields. Maybe she could get married again—if she could find a bachelor generous enough to take on her three children. Some of them were desperate enough.

"Be sure to talk to Ichiro-san," I said as he set off in his black suit to the Mikami taxi stand. I hated nagging him, but the men were so afraid of making a scene.

When he didn't return by dusk, I *oppa*ed Joji and paced the veranda. I thought of going to the taxi stand on Main Street. But his lateness was a good sign. He was enjoying himself after receiving the $300. We would need it, with another child in my belly. He finally came home after dark.

"Oh, you're late; you must be tired."

"I let Mikami go. I caught a ride home." He sat on the veranda and took off his shoes.

"Did you talk to him?"

He nodded in the dark.

"What did he say?" I followed him into the parlor.

"He said his brother had charged goods under other people's names, people who weren't even friends of the family. He said he had to pay them first."

"How much did that amount to?"

"About $300."

"How many of them were there?"

He shrugged. "Six, seven."

"That's less than $50 per family. Ours alone is $300! So is he going to take out another *tanomoshi?*"

"He said he's still got eight months to go on the present *tanomoshi.*"

"Then he'll be forming another *tanomoshi* in eight months?"

"No."

"Then how does he expect to pay us?"

"He said he got into debt just paying off the others. He can't go further into debt."

"Why not? He's a *luna*. He gets good pay! He has only one child!"

"He said he had to pay the outsiders first; he didn't have money to pay me."

"And you still consider him your best friend?"

He nodded.

"You consider him your best friend, but he doesn't even think of you as a friend! Nobody would treat a friend like this!"

"Shut up!" he yelled.

"It's not as if he's your boss or father."

"He chose me for his steam plow gang."

"You owe him for that?"

"Shut up!"

"Well, at least we won't pay him the $30 we owe him!"

Why can't he blow up at Ichiro the way he does at me? I thought. I'd thought Ichiro was handsome in a gangly way, but now all I could think of were his awkwardness and oversized head. It was a good thing we didn't live in Kahana. I'd probably say something to him. No, I couldn't embarrass Isao. "He can't control his wife," people would laugh. Besides, my vaunted courage turned into stage fright every time I confronted anybody outside the family. But exposure was the only recourse. They had to be shamed into living up to their obligations. Suffering in silence only covered up for them.

The debt was now $200 to Mr. Kanda, $300 charged by Kawai Jiro, $100 of our own bills, then $300 in sundry expenses—Mikami taxi, boarding Toshio and Joji, not to mention $1,000 in obligations and bills Father Takao had left us.

"We're over $1,900 in debt when it should be only $400."

"Don't worry," Isao said with a flick of the wrist.

I wrote Aunt Kitano that I was expecting. She wrote that I should see Dr. Hall right away.

Medical care used to be free on the plantation, but now it cost $5, and the birth, $50.

Shizuko-san said, "Dr. Hall says you should abort the child."

"But I'd be worthless if I could have only two children."

"But you'll be endangering your own life," she said.

"Hmmmm . . . I'll have to think about it."

"You have to make up your mind soon."

I asked Isao, "What shall I do? It's as if they're telling me I can't have another child. Aunt Kitano must've thought the same thing."

"Do you feel strong enough?"

"Yes. Thanks to Kula, I'm back to my old self."

"What do you want to do?"

"I'd like to have at least three children. You know what I think? I had such difficult births the last two times because you gave the boys such fierce names. I'll be all right this time if you give the child a gentle name if it's a boy."

I didn't go back to see Dr. Hall. I felt stronger than in my previous pregnancies. But now I had a three year old and a one year old underfoot. Toshio had changed so much since I returned form Kula. He acted up more, begging to be pampered. Joji, by contrast, was so undemanding.

I girded myself like a samurai readying for battle. I rested as much as I could and ate lots of vegetables and Hawaiian fruits, as I'd done at Kula. I couldn't have meat or potatoes, but I had lots of fish and rice. I listed all our debts in my ledger and wrote a short biography of the family. Just in case.

I was composed when my labor started. Isao got the taxi.

"Don't worry," I told him.

I felt guilty for not having gone back to tell them I wasn't going to abort the child. It would've been the polite thing to do. What if Dr. Hall were proven right?

But my labor lasted only an hour. Dr. Hall laughed, and Shizuko-san translated, "Tell her I won't give her any more advice."

Shizuko-san was an older, unmarried nisei woman. The hospital had only one registered nurse, a *haole* who supervised the couple dozen nisei nurses' aides. People said Shizuko-san was better than the interns and had done emergency appendectomies in Dr. Hall's absence.

Isao named him Kiyoshi, or "gentle one."

I was fine, but now Kiyoshi was the sickly one. He weighed only four pounds. He couldn't digest my milk and cried and cried. Was I going to lose him as I'd done Kazue? I went back to the hospital. Dr. Hall and Shizuko-san gave me a milk-free formula. Kiyoshi's stool got harder and his appetite improved.

Thirty days after his birth, on *hi-ake* day, Mrs. Koga and Mrs. Oshiro brought their belated birth gifts. Kiyoshi was now seven pounds.

Mrs. Oshiro covered her mouth and said, "We have a confession to make. He was so puny we thought he wasn't going to live. So we said to each other, 'We might have to give him another gift a month later. Let's wait a month, and if he dies, we'll just give him a death gift.'"

We laughed and laughed till tears came to our eyes.

Isao was so proud. "I'm three for three." He flicked his hand.

"Elder sister Tomi has *four* sons," I teased.

16 · The Great Earthquake

The $25 a month Mr. Nishida paid Isao couldn't cover our expenses. We were going $20 into debt every month.

Then Father Takao wrote from Tokyo. "We can hardly keep up with the company's demands. I'll be needing both your hands if the business keeps up . . ."

It excited and depressed me. I'd be seeing my mother, my sister, and Toru! But I remembered the tofu and pigs and how badly Father Takao had treated Isao. "He's aware only of what's owed him, never what he owes," Aunt Kitano had said. I missed her. There was nobody in Pepelau I could talk to. Madame Kanai, the wife of the reverend at church, fussed over us like a mother hen, but I could never discuss family business with her.

"We still have all our debts. I don't see how we can go," I said.

"We can pay them while in Japan," Isao said.

"On $5 a month allowance? You should tell him about our $2,000 debt, $1,000 of which we inherited from him. He even took Toshio's candies."

"We have to go if he calls us."

* * *

My troubles were here and now. We needed money. *What can I do?* There was no demand for kimonos, or maybe people didn't know I could sew kimonos.

Our landlord, Mr. Ando, was a *kibei* tinsmith. He was a skinny older man. His wife, Mie-chan, was a young, vivacious nisei. I thanked her for alerting Isao about Toshio. Included in the rental fee was the use of their bathhouse. She built the fire for the bath and was always so considerate.

The Oshiros, who also shared the bath, were friendly like Mie-chan. He was a jovial big man and his wife was so good-natured. They were childless and had adopted their nephew to carry on their line. I went to his tailor shop one afternoon with my three boys, Kiyoshi strapped to my back.

"Can I sit here and watch you and your assistants sew? I'd like to learn how to sew pants and shirts. I have a sewing machine and can do smocking, but I know only kimonos."

"Of course," he said, and brought out a chair for me.

I sat there day after day and watched Mr. Oshiro and his two assistants sew. Mr. Oshiro would point out and show things to me. Mrs. Oshiro would bring out candies for the boys and tea for me. Shirts and trousers were so much easier than kimonos. The secret was in the measuring, drafting, and cutting. The machine did the rest.

After a month Mr. Oshiro let me sew some trousers and shirts on one of his machines. Then he let me take home pieces to sew on my treadle Singer. In another month he was paying me for the piecework. After three months he said I was good enough to take orders on my own. I bought an electric motor on credit to drive my Singer as they did at the tailor shop, and I told all our friends, "*Tanomimasu*, I'll be able to sew your trousers and shirts cheaply."

I waited and waited, but nobody came. I bought bolts of cloth on credit from Koga Store and sewed the boys and Isao pants and shirts just to keep in practice. I kept announcing that I did shirts and trousers very cheaply, but getting the first order was so difficult. People didn't know what I could do. How was I to establish a reputation if nobody came? The only jobs I got were the piecework Mr. Oshiro gave me.

In June we got the dreaded letter from Tokyo. "I'm looking for a bigger house to expand my operations. I'll send for you as soon as I find it. You need not bring any gifts. Just come with the clothes on your backs . . ." Father Takao wrote.

It depressed me. I visualized all of us working sixteen hours a day, making paper wrappers for monosodium glutamate. Ten of us would be imprisoned in this house, working our fingers to the bone just to make Father Takao a success. It'd be worse than tofu and pigs. I wouldn't be able to run to the cane field or cry on Aunt Kitano's shoulder. And what about Toshio, Joji, and Kiyoshi?

Two months went by. *Maybe he's changed his mind,* I thought. Or the business had slowed down. Most likely, though, he hadn't been able to find a bigger house.

"You should write him and say we can't come for a while," I kept saying to Isao. We had to refuse beforehand. We were taught in grade school, "The debt to the parents is deeper than the ocean, higher than the mountains, and can never be repaid." They'd given you life and cared for you when you were a helpless infant. So repayment meant sacrificing your own life? What about your children's lives?

"You have to write him," I nagged. Isao seemed paralyzed.

The last day of August was hot and humid. Back Street is only a block from the ocean, but there's hardly any breeze. The trade winds blow down from Kahana and out into the ocean at Kaanapali and leave Pepelau sweltering in a cove. You have to stand right next to the water to feel any sea breeze.

It was so muggy I could barely cope with the children. Then Mrs. Koga came running to the veranda, then Mrs. Oshiro, then Mie-chan, all breathlessly announcing, "Tokyo was leveled by an earthquake!"

"Do you have relatives in Tokyo?" they asked.

At dusk Mr. Kashima delivered the little scrolls of Japanese newspapers from Honolulu and said, "The whole city has collapsed; there're over 100,000 dead."

Isao was at sea and didn't come home till a couple of days later.

"Over half of the city has burned," he said. "It triggered a tsunami, which hit Sagami Gulf."

"Should you write?"

"Where? Most likely they've been burned out."

"What about your uncle? Doesn't he live in a better district?"

"Yes. His house was of reinforced concrete."

The *Nippu Jiji* arrived by steamship three days late. The casualties kept climbing. One hundred forty thousand were dead, 300,000 injured.

"He'll get his *bachi* some day." I remembered Aunt Kitano's words. But an earthquake was not a punishment; it was a catastrophe. Twenty years of frugality and toil went *pffft!* in seconds. Poor Father Takao; he was born unlucky.

Two weeks later, we got a letter from my mother. They were all well in Fukuoka. A few days later Father Takao's letter said they'd all survived, but he'd lost everything. He needed at least $800 to begin anew. How much could we send him?

Isao went to Kahana and borrowed $100 from Mr. Kanda.

17 · Konomi Maru

One day Isao came home all excited. "This is my chance. Mr. Tokunaga is selling his boat."

"But you've been an apprentice for only two years," I said.

"It's now or never. It's like swimming. You have to jump in, and the sooner the better."

"But you're so impulsive."

"I won't have another chance like this. Tokunaga's boat is thirty-two feet, one horse power, four knots. It's the second largest in Pepelau. That means I can go beyond Nishida's range."

"But you don't know any fishing grounds."

"I'll have to find them."

"Is Mr. Tokunaga going to show you *his* fishing grounds?"

"He can't. He had a stroke."

"How much is it?"

"$800."

"Where are you getting the money?"

"Tani Fish Market will loan me $400 if I give them first choice of my catch. Then I'll borrow $400 from Kanda."

Two thousand dollars plus $800! How were we ever going to pay off $2,800?!

He renamed the sampan *Konomi Maru*, after Mt. Konomi, a hill his family had owned in their ancestral village.

Mrs. Nishida cooked chicken *heka* to celebrate the occasion.

"You don't have to worry about him," Mr. Nishida said. "He respects the sea."

I quickly learned fishing was worse than gambling. Bait, ice, and fuel cost money. So you could work all day and night and still lose money. Whenever he went beyond the range of the others, he came back empty. He could break even only by fishing in the common grounds. It was no different than working for Mr. Nishida.

One night he got up as if to go out to sea.

"What are you doing? It's early yet," I said, and followed him to the veranda where he kept his working clothes.

"I promised somebody I'd take him to Lanai," he whispered.

"At midnight? Why can't it wait till morning?" I followed him back into the kitchen.

"He's running away."

"From the police?"

"From his creditors. They're seizing all his belongings tomorrow."

"Who is he?"

"He's a *hapa*."

"He's not even Japanese, and you're doing this for him? Do you owe him?"

"He said he'll show me some *onaga* grounds."

"How can he if his boat has been seized?"

"He'll tell it to me."

"Have him write it down."

"You don't write down secrets."

"What's his name?"

"Baker."

"Just him?"

"He has a wife and two children."

"I'll fix you lunch."

"No, I don't need any. Turn off the light," he said, and sneaked out. I watched him disappear into the dark.

I went back into the tent-like gauze net that covered the whole room. Often in the morning there'd be a fat mosquito barely able to fly. Toshio or Joji would clap it, splattering the red blood onto their palms.

I couldn't sleep. It's twelve miles to Lanai. At four knots an hour, it'll take three hours to get there and three to get back. Besides, he'll have to load the belongings onto his skiff and row to where his boat is anchored a good fifty yards away. He'll need at least two trips on the skiff with a family of four and their belongings. He should forget the belongings and take only the necessities. Why did the *hapa* ask Isao? Maybe the others had refused. Only Mr. Iwai had a larger boat, but he was a stubborn old man. The *hapa* must've known Isao was softhearted. What can they charge him with if he's caught? Helping a debtor escape? Will they throw him in jail? Will they confiscate the boat?

I must've dozed off. The footsteps were on the veranda, not in my head. I rushed out. Dawn was breaking.

"Pack my lunch; I'm going out," he said.

"I'll have to cook the rice."

"Just pack the cold rice. I'll cook some at sea."

"Why don't you rest today; you must be tired."

"No, I have to go now while my memory's fresh."

"But you haven't slept."

"I can go days without sleep when I'm doing what I love. Besides, I need about ten hours to get to the fishing ground."

"Where?"

"The other side of Kahoolawe."

"That far? Will you be out of sight of land?"

"No. I'd get lost if I did."

"When will you be back?'

"Five days."

"Five days?!" Even with Mr. Nishida he'd been out at most three nights.

"It's a ground only Iwai and I can reach."

I fried a *paka* in Crisco and packed cold rice in his round aluminum lunch pail.

"Be sure to get enough fuel," I said.

It was a good thing I had so much to do, feeding the children, bathing them, washing the diapers. He was safe as long as he was in the confines of Molokai, Lanai, and Kahoolawe. Going beyond scared me. What if it's so deep he can't anchor? What if the anchor rope broke while he slept?

The house felt so empty. We had an early supper and went to the wharf to watch the sunset. The sky turned a brilliant red and the sun dipped into the liquid gold.

"*Oyasumi nasai, Otoosan,*" I said, and Toshio and Joji repeated, "Good night, Father."

The fifth day was the worst. I ran out to the veranda every time I heard footsteps. I fixed an early supper and hurried to the wharf with the children. I scanned the horizon till it got dark. *Something's happened!* My heart wouldn't stop fluttering. What if his engine broke down? There were several one-day sampans, small boats that couldn't pack enough ice or fuel to stay out overnight. The fishermen would form a search party the next morning whenever one of them didn't return. Mr. Mitsui never came back. The search party could find no trace of his boat. I went to Tani Fish Market on Front Street and asked Mr. Tani to organize a search party in the morning.

"Did he say where was he going?"

"Beyond Kahoolawe."

"Hmmm . . . nobody goes there," he said, getting me more worried.

I couldn't sleep. I'd get up and pace as if to hasten the dawn. Then at first light I fed the children and took them to the wharf. Mr. Tani and half a dozen fishermen were already there.

"*Tanomimasu.*" I bowed to them.

Everybody would search toward Kahoolawe. Mr. Iwai would go outward for a day and a half and search for a day. The others would have to search within their respective ranges.

"*Tanomimasu, tanomimasu.*" I kept bowing.

Then just as they were getting on their skiffs to row to their sampans, I spied a dot on the horizon.

"There he is! There he is!"

We all waited and crowded at the front of the wharf when he came through the channel. He waved, smiling, as he turned left. Then he skipped like a dancer to the engine room. He anchored the boat in front of the sea wall on Front Street, unloaded his barley bags onto the skiff, and rowed past the wharf to the mooring in front of the courthouse. We crowded around the beach as he pushed the skiff onto the sand. He had six barley bags full of brilliant red fish. The spectators oohed when he opened a bag and held up a big red *onaga*, its milky white guts popping out of its mouth like a little balloon.

"The engine konked out on my way back. Luckily I was in the calm waters off the *pali*. It took me the whole night to fix it. I was more worried about the ice melting and my catch spoiling." He dismissed it with a flick of a wrist above his head.

No other fisherman had a boat big enough to follow Isao to the fishing grounds except Mr. Iwai, who was too old and set in his ways. Mr. Nishida had thrown a knife at a *hapa's* boat that had tried to follow him to *his* fishing grounds. Even then everybody soon found out where it was.

"I've bested Nishida in a month!" Isao bragged.

18 · The Onaga King

The next birth was easy. Aunt Kitano delivered her and saved us $50. Isao named her Takako, after Father Takao. A week later the American government passed a law barring Japanese immigrants. I felt sad. There'd be no more picture brides. "It's a slap in our face," Isao said.

Our house was now a nursery. It was just as well I didn't get orders for pants and shirts. Coping with four children took up all my time. Luckily, the iceman deposited the daily block of ice right into our icebox, and the vegetable man, who also sold tofu and miso, stopped every afternoon in front of the tailor shop.

Isao and his *onaga* catches were the talk of the town. He drew a crowd every time he rowed his skiff to the beach in front of the courthouse. They called him the *onaga* king.

"I'd have to work eight months on the plantation to make what I made this month!" he'd say.

Each time he had a $100 catch, he'd bring home six "baseballs," ice cream covered with chocolate and wrapped in foil, costing 10 cents each. "*Beisuboru, beisuboru,*" the boys would say as they ran to greet his cart.

"Fish are like people," he'd explain. "They live in communities in the valleys. So I have to be exact where I drop my lines. A few feet off and my lines would fall on the ridges instead of the valleys, and I wouldn't get a single bite. I line up two landmarks the way you aim a rifle. Then I bait all ten hooks and drop the line over the side. I roll a

Bull Durham and smoke it to the end. When I finish it, it's time to haul up the line. I can tell immediately how many bites I have. The *onaga* swim upward and lighten my pull. The more fish, the lighter the load. Their guts pop out of their mouths. That's why they make the best sashimi. Their flesh is firm from being seventy fathoms down. That's why they bring the best price. You don't know what it's like eating live sashimi with hot rice after a day of fishing. The setting sun turns the sea into shimmering gold. Sitting on the deck, I feel like a feudal lord. The ocean is my domain, the *onaga* my hidden gold . . ."

He loved fish so much, he made a meal out of rice and sashimi. He'd bring home the leftover prawns he used for bait and slice them into sashimi. He was a beautiful slicer. Once he brought home a fugu. He cut out the poisonous sac and cooked it.

"No!" I yelled when he offered me some.

I forbade the children to taste it. We sat across the table and watched him eat. The poison was so strong you dropped dead on the spot, they said.

"Don't worry." He slurped more noisily than usual.

I still felt queasy when he stayed out four nights. "Please keep him safe," I prayed to Kami-sama, the Methodist God.

When the sea was rough, the boats would circle outside the breakers and wait for a lull in the waves. Boats coming through the channel headed straight for the wharf. On the right was a large pile of rocks, the ruins of an old seawall. So the boats had to turn left sharply as soon as they got through the channel. Once Mr. Terauchi entered the channel too late. A big wave rose behind him and pushed his boat straight toward the wharf. He turned left at the last moment and the wave hit him on the side and capsized the boat. Miraculously, he escaped unhurt.

"You don't have to worry about me. I respect the sea," Isao always said. But I held my breath each time he came chugging slowly through the channel while another series of waves began to build behind him. He always waved as he made his turn. "There's Father, there's Father!" I'd say, and the children would wave back. When the catch was good, he'd skip from the stern to the engine room.

It must've been lonesome being at sea for four nights. He couldn't stop talking when he got back. "The ocean air is so clean. Even your sweat smells clean. There's nobody around to annoy you. Some nights I fish for *aji* by torchlight. Except for the stars, mine is the only light in the entire universe. Then far off I see a light. I'm positive there's no boat there."

"What if it's a ghost?" The Kanakas had so many ghost stories.

He laughed. "I'll ask it to show me where the fish are."

He was suddenly in demand everywhere. Madame Kanai asked him to paint the backdrops for the samurai plays she put on at the Methodist church. She wanted him to act in the plays, but he didn't have time for the rehearsals. When the Japan theater troupes came to the Nippon Theater on Back Street, Mr. Masuda, who owned the concession at the theater, asked him to paint *their* backdrops. He'd take a couple days off and lay the large canvas on the floor of the reception room at the Masuda Hotel on Back Street and paint for two to three days and get paid $20. We'd get free tickets, and Mr. Masuda would give the children free shaved ice at the theater.

When the Japan sumo wrestlers came to perform at the ring that had been set up next to the mill, they asked Isao to be the announcer. He loved it. Dressed in *hakama* and clapping the wooden sticks, he'd sing out in the quirky Kabuki intonation, "*Higa-aashi, Higonishiki, Higonishiki* (east is Higonishiki). *Ni-iishi, Taka-no-mori, Taka-no-mori* (west is Takanomori). *Higashi wa Higonishiki! Nishi wa Taka-no-mori!*"

It was like he was on stage. He wasn't the slightest bit nervous, and he remembered all the fancy sumo names. Afterward he got a 100-pound bag of rice, which cost $5.

He said to the children, "Do you know why they say, 'east and west,' and not 'south and north'?" And he brought out his brush and ink slab and wrote on an old newspaper.

南に北

"*Minami ni kita* (south and north) can also be written"

皆見に來た

"*Mina mini kita* (They all came to watch). Do you see?"

The children seemed puzzled. So was I. The spectators didn't sit only south and north, as he implied, but also behind the wrestlers on east and west. *What do you mean?* I was going to say when I realized, *Oh, it's just another one of his puns.* Besides, he wanted to show off his calligraphy, which was more magnificient than his father's.

He and four friends formed a *hyohtan-kai* (calabash club). They'd drink and party once every four months. I had to prepare the party foods when Isao played host, but I didn't mind. They were celebrating success. All five of them, including Mr. Oshiro, the tailor, were young men who were doing well on their own. We bought our first furniture, a *tansu*.

I worried less with each succeeding child, but I was ever watchful. Takako was an easy child with good bowel movements. But some days everything went wrong. All of them were underfoot, Toshio picked on Joji, Kiyoshi on Takako, and the bawling never stopped. One day Kiyoshi threw another tantrum. I grabbed him and stuffed him into a *tansu* drawer. He screamed even more, then stopped dead. I pulled open the drawer in a panic. He was all right. *Why did I do that?* I wondered later. He was special. But I wasn't going to have him turn out like Toshio.

I had to be alert even while sewing. Did Takako crawl out to the veranda? Did one of the boys wander out to the street? One of them would vanish as soon as I turned my back. But it was such a pleasure to watch them grow. I bathed them in shifts now, Joji and Toshio first, then the others with me later.

September brought relief. Toshio entered kindergarten, which was across from Koga Store. A tall picket fence surrounded the large school yard, and I'd take the children to play there occasionally to get away from my "nursery." One of Toshio's teachers was Mrs. Goo, a nisei married to a Chinese storekeeper. One day the free milk the children got had soured. Mrs. Goo accompanied Toshio to the house after school and explained in impeccable Japanese that the little bottle of milk was still drinkable if boiled first.

After American kindergarten, Toshio went to the language school kindergarten run by Madame Kanai. Kahana didn't even have a kindergarten after Madame Morimoto left for Honolulu a couple of months ago.

I was also getting used to the tropics. It was only natural for children to go barefoot. It saved on shoes. And wearing your shirttails out was cooler. All the women wore loose-fitting cotton dresses. Yet I felt nostalgic every fall. I missed the autumn colors. But the winters here were so pleasant. I shivered every time I thought of the winters back home. The small charcoal brazier barely warmed your hands and feet. You stopped shivering only in the hot bath.

Life was simple here. We ate fish, rice, miso, and pickles. The only other expenses were cloth for clothing, zoris, tea, soy sauce, cabbage, Crisco, and the ingredients for the beer Isao brewed in the kitchen.

Nights when Isao was out at sea, I actually missed his snoring. There'd been moments I enjoyed the tingling sensation spreading from my thighs. I enjoyed his embraces, which happened only when he made love.

On some Sundays Isao would take Mr. Pombo fishing. He was the machine shop *luna* in Kahana, and he always brought a couple loaves of homemade Portuguese bread. "Porogee *pan!* Porogee *pan!*" the children would squeal. Isao insisted that Mr. Pombo wear no pullovers. All shirts and shorts should have buttons in the front to be pulled off easily if one were thrown overboard.

"Oyama, you're a man of good character," Mr. Pombo said after a couple of beers in the kitchen. "All your children get their character from you. They get their heads from the Mrs."

Isao laughed, but afterward he said angrily, "What does he take me for, a *lolo?*"

"He's complimenting you for being well prepared," I said.

When Mr. Koga closed his store and returned to Japan, many owed him money. Isao probably was the only one who kept sending him money orders.

No news from Japan was good news. Our debt was now down to $1,000. If this kept up, we'd be able to return to Japan in five to six years. It would be just in time, too. The children were losing their Japanese-ness.

In November, when the maple leaves turn scarlet, Sadao Ono, Aunt Kitano's youngest child, returned from Japan. He'd been ten when his father took him there. Now he was a handsome, tall five feet seven inches. He had Koso's fluidity and gentleness. And the same high nose and symmetrical features. The other half of the family had the high cheekbones and button nose of Mother Haru and my own mother.

Sadao brought a studio portrait of himself, Father Takao, Mother Haru, Chiyako (now a beautiful twenty-one), Kingo, nineteen, in his cropped haircut and black school uniform, and demure Masako, thirteen. Father Takao and Mother Haru looked old and tired. He was now an interpreter at the Canadian Consulate in Tokyo. I wondered if they paid him enough to support the family. I worried about Chiyako's dowry. Would he be able to marry her off? The women wore beautiful kimonos, so they must be doing all right, I thought.

We should send them our portrait to celebrate Sadao's arrival, Isao said. I sewed white shirts and short pants for the boys and white dresses for me and Takako. Then I bought socks and Keds shoes for the boys and stockings and shoes for me and Takako.

"We're taking *shashin,* so you have to cut your hair," Kiyoshi said to little Takako, and cut off a handful of hair from her bangs. I laughed and laughed, but it wasn't funny. I oiled and combed and recombed her hair to cover the rat bite. Aunt Kitano, her husband, and Sadao met us at Nakamoto Studio on Front Street. It was a handsome photo, the men in suits standing behind Aunt Kitano and me, who were seated in ornate chairs with legs that curved into animal claws, and the children standing next to us. We all looked like kin except for Mr. Kitano, who had a pointed face and floppy ears. We were a good-looking family.

Isao wrote them about his *Konomi Maru* and the success he was having.

"Don't tell them about your $100 days. They'll ask you for money," I said.

I also sent a photo to my mother. My last image of them was when I'd said goodbye at the train station. *What do they look like now? Why haven't they sent any photos?*

Sadao-san went to live with his mother and stepfather in Kahana and got a job at the plantation carpenter shop.

The only sad event of the year happened on Christmas eve. The Taisho emperor, Yoshihito, died at age forty-seven. He'd suffered a stroke and had been sickly for so long. The new emperor called his reign Showa, or "bright peace." His birthday was April twenty-ninth, but it didn't matter. Nobody celebrated the emperor's birthday in Pepelau.

19 · The Accident

Takako entered kindergarten in September 1928. *Time to myself at last,* I thought. I remembered the walks to and from my sewing classes. Solitude was so relaxing. Constantly reading other people's minds and anticipating their wishes was so exhausting.

A few days later Mrs. Oshiro came running to the veranda and whispered, "Oyama-san, they've just caught the boy who kidnapped and killed the little white boy! He's a nisei named Fukunaga Yutaka! I just heard it over the radio!"

"It's not some mistake?!"

"It's no mistake! He even confessed and asked for the death penalty!"

I couldn't sew for the rest of the day. My skin literally burned with shame. It was as if Toshio or Joji had done it. I never had time to read the *Nippu Jiji* before. Now I broke the seals and read the back issues. None of the articles even hinted that the kidnapper and murderer might be Japanese. It would have nothing to do with me if the culprit were a *gaijin*, but how could a Japanese do such a thing? *"Nihonjin no kuse ni,"* we say; "in spite of being Japanese" how could you do it? Killing your own was bad enough, but a *haole!* They were like the samurai and nobility of feudal times. Commoners had to walk several steps behind so as not to step on their shadows. How could he not know his place?

The paper several days later had a picture of Myles Yutaka Fukunaga. He didn't look criminal. He could've been any nisei. I vomited the next morning. *It could be just an upset stomach,* I thought. I'd missed my monthlies before.

The trial began on October third, the day after he was caught. On October fifth he was sentenced to be hanged. His lawyers appealed, claiming he was insane.

It was during the trial that I found out I was not alone. I had another baby in my belly.

"They should hang him right away! He's a disgrace to the Japanese community!" Isao said when he came home from sea.

"But he must be insane. Why else would he kill the boy when he could have held out for the ransom?"

"So why did he pick on the boy? His father was the vice president of the company that forcibly collected the rent from his mother. So it had to be revenge. But instead of avenging himself on the father, he picks on the son. He's a coward!"

"But he wanted the money to send his parents back to Japan."

"First he tries suicide and disgraces his parents. Then he tries to act heroic and disgraces them even more."

"That's why he's insane."

Several weeks later Kiyoshi said his teacher, Mrs. Woods, was going to take the class to the plantation dairy in Honokawai. Mrs. Woods was an artist, and they were going to draw pictures of cows. She was the wife of the manager of the large plantation store on Front Street, which was why she could get a plantation truck for the ten-mile trip. The other two first-grade classes were jealous, Kiyoshi said.

"So I'll be going directly to language school," he said.

Liliuokalani Grade School was from 8:00 A.M. to 1:30 P.M., and the Japanese children who lived in town went home first before going on to their respective language schools. The Buddhists went to the Hongwanji School at the east end of town beyond Liliuokalani, and the Christians went to *kyokai* at the west end of town.

Takako came home at half past eleven, had lunch, and set off for her kindergarten language school. At about two o'clock Joji and Toshio came home, had soda crackers and jelly, and left. It was just another day.

Then about half past two Joji came running into the parlor with unwashed feet. "Mother! Mother! Kiyo was run over by a car!"

"Where?!"

"At *kyokai.* There was blood all over!"

"Is he alive?"

"I don't know! They took him to the plantation hospital!"

I ran and ran, stumbling, panting, cheeks puffed, nearly blacking out, my heart pounding in my ears.

Toshio was at the entrance. "He's in the operating room. He broke both legs."

"Was he awake?"

"They say he was unconscious."

Toshio held my elbow. "Sit down."

"How did it happen?"

"Mrs. Woods stopped the truck in front of the Methodist church to let the *kyokai* students off. Kiyo ran across the street, and a car hit him."

"Who was driving?"

"A Kanaka boy."

"Madame Kanai scolded Mrs. Woods for not supervising the children. She sat in the cab with the driver and let the children jump off the truck. I beat up Masaru Shinozuka because he said Kiyo had it coming because he was too cocky. He was racing somebody across the street, and I guess he won. He was the only one hit."

Michie Takashima, a nurse's aide from Kahana, came out. "Kiyo-chan's legs were broken. Luckily, they're simple fractures."

We sat on the wooden bench outside the operating room and waited. He came out on a gurney four hours later. Both legs were in casts, and he reeked of chloroform.

Mr. Kunichika, the anesthesiologist, said, "He'll be all right."

"When will he wake up?"

"In four to six hours."

They put him in an empty ward with four beds.

"I'll stay. You go home and cook for the others," I said.

"I don't know how," Toshio said.

"There's some old rice in the safe. Also some pickled cabbage. And there's some *paka* in the icebox. Fry them in Crisco."

"I hate fish," he said.

"Fry yourself two eggs."

"When is Papa coming home?"

"Tomorrow."

Toshio started to leave. "You know, we're bad luck. There're only a dozen cars in Pepelau and one hits him."

The nisei nurse's aide working the night shift brought me a tray of food, but I wasn't hungry. At nine o'clock the lights were turned off, and I sat in the dark, listening to his breathing. There was no doubt now. Another baby was growing in my belly. Was it to be Kiyoshi's substitute? Whenever someone died, another was born in his place.

"Please, Kami-sama, help us," I kept praying. The Christian God was so intangible. You couldn't offer Him food or show Him pictures of your newborn son. It was like praying to air.

It was past midnight when I heard him whimper, "Mother, Mother . . . "

"Oh, Kiyoshi."

"My legs hurt."

"They're in casts. You were run over by a car. Please *gaman*."

"It stinks."

"It's the chloroform."

*　*　*

He was his old self in a couple of days.

"He'll be on his feet in no time," Shizue-san interpreted for Dr. Hall.

Isao carried him home after three weeks. We bought a second-hand bed and placed it next to the window in the parlor.

Mrs. Woods brought her class to see him. They were mostly Japanese.

"*Dohzoh*, please don't bother," I said when she tried to take off her shoes at the veranda. The house was dirty anyway. Besides, all the children were barefoot.

Her auburn hair was in bangs and her skin pearl white. She was tall and wore a flowing coral dress of silk. I felt so awed; my neck turned into jelly when I tried to look at her.

"It's Mrs. Woods' fault," Madame Kanai said. "She should've supervised the children. She just sat there in the cab."

"She meant well," I said. "She wanted to save the *kyokai* children a walk back from American school," I said. *We shouldn't carp so soon after the Myles Fukunaga incident,* I thought.

"But would she have been so nonchalant if the children were white?"

Madame Kanai spoke fluent English and acted as interpreter for the congregation. While all the Japanese women wore plain cotton dresses, Madame Kanai dressed in flowing long-sleeved silk dresses and bell-shaped or broad-brimmed hats. She was a foot taller than her husband, and she glided when she walked. Reverend Kanai, on the other hand, was short and stiff like a stick. He had graduated from Columbia University in New York, but his English sounded as bad as Isao's.

The sixteen-year-old driver of the car had no license or insurance. Clifford Palama was a tall, skinny five feet ten inches. He had curly black hair, big round eyes, and a gentle, sad face. Isao had threatened to sue him and his family, but Mrs. Palama cried and begged him not to. In return Clifford would work for Isao without pay.

Isao bought a cot, and Clifford slept in the vacant Koga warehouse. He'd come and talk to Kiyoshi each time he came back from sea. One night after they'd returned from sea, he asked if he could skip supper and go see his mother, who lived about a mile west of *kyokai.* His eyes were red and swollen.

At supper Isao said, "I'm going to let him go. He's no help. He cries all the time."

"But how are we going to pay Kiyoshi's hospital bill?"

"He's no help. He only gets in the way."

"But won't he get used to it?"

"He's only a child."

"But what about the hospital bill?"

"We'll manage somehow."

"You're too easy on our debtors. I wouldn't mind it if we were rich."

That night Isao walked to Clifford's home to tell his mother that Clifford need not help with the fishing anymore. The next morning Clifford brought bags full of mangoes, papayas, and bananas for Kiyoshi.

"Hey, Kiyo, you eat now; you eat plenty, eh!" he said, full of smiles.

I bought a side of ham and cooked Kiyoshi ham and eggs every morning. I explained to the others that he needed this special food so that he could walk without a limp. Mrs. Woods came once a week to help him with his lessons.

It rained every day after New Year's day. For a whole week Isao unrolled the tatami mat in the parlor and worked on his lines and hooks. During the second week he'd go out before dark with his lunch pail and come home about nine o'clock.

"Did anybody else go out?" I asked each time.

The storm and the Kona winds didn't let up. Coconuts fell everywhere. The wind knocked down several *kiawe* trees. I wore my *haori* and put an extra futon on Kiyoshi. The third week was the same. Isao would come home late in the morning and go into the bedroom to read. A couple of times he didn't come home till suppertime.

Then the rain and gales stopped. I fixed Isao's lunch, and he set off before dawn. He came home about nine o'clock, his lunch bag slung over his shoulder.

"Oh, you didn't go out today?"

"The current's too fast, and the wind's too strong."

"It's not windy here."

"The sea's full of white caps." He kicked off his slippers.

"How are we going to pay Kiyoshi's hospital bill?"

"You only lose money if you go out on a day like this." He headed for the bedroom with a book.

I sat at the sewing machine to sew another shirt for Mr. Oshiro. "Did anybody go out today?"

"No."

"If fishing is so uncertain, maybe we should return to the plantation."

"What did you say?" I said when he didn't answer.

"Nothing!"

When Takako came home from kindergarten, I fixed lunch and called, "Come, have a lunch of rice and pickled radish. We can't afford anything more with Father staying home every day."

I took Kiyoshi his tray, and Isao, Takako, and I sat down to lunch in the kitchen.

"I wonder if the stores will extend us any more credit? Why can't you catch anything on a day like this? The sun is shining, the sky is blue," I said.

"*Baka!* Can't you understand? How many times do I have to tell you! It's foolish to go out on a day like this! You use up $5 worth of fuel, bait, and ice, and catch nothing!"

"But the weather is fine. I can't understand a man not working when the weather is fine."

"But fish don't bite when the current's fast!"

I stood up to refill the dish with pickled radish. "But how are we to pay Kiyoshi's hospital bill? Maybe you should quit fishing. We only go deeper into debt. How can we survive when you haven't worked for a whole month?"

"Chikusho!"

It happened so fast that I felt no pain. Then I burst into tears. Takako bawled. He'd thrown his bowl of rice at me and stalked out. Takako ran to Kiyoshi in the parlor.

"Father threw his bowl of rice at Mother!" Takako screamed.

"Go ask her if she's hurt," Kiyoshi said.

"Does it hurt? Shall I call the doctor?" Takako came back as I rubbed my hip. She picked up the pieces of china and rice from the floor.

"No." I stifled a laugh. "Finish your meal."

"I'm finished. Mother, can I go now to kindergarten? I'll be late if I don't leave," Takako said.

It had been so sudden, this turnaround in fishing. At dusk I went through the motions of fixing supper, wondering if he'd show up. We'd run out of fish and now ate rice, tofu, miso soup, and pickles.

Isao came home for supper, but he said hardly anything. I kept my mouth shut. Anything I'd say would end up as nagging.

"Komban wa, Oyama-san," a melodious voice called later that night.

"Please don't take off your shoes; our house is so dirty," I said, surprised to see Madame Kanai.

She talked briefly with Kiyoshi, then asked if she could talk to Isao and me in the kitchen.

"I was worried," she said. "Taka-chan told me that Father threw a bowl of rice at Mother and hit her right here." She pointed to her hip.

I covered my mouth and laughed so hard tears came to my eyes. Isao laughed, heh-heh-heh.

"Oh, that Taka-chan, she's such a tattle-tale! It was just a husband-wife spat! It was nothing! She shouldn't have bothered you, *okusama!"* I said.

Isao scratched his head and sucked his breath. "We can't do anything in front of the children."

"Oh, I'm glad it wasn't anything serious," Madame Kanai said, and we all laughed.

Madame Kanai told a story once at the monthly meeting of the women's club, which I could attend only occasionally. A wife was carrying a tray of dishes and fell. "Did you break any?" her husband yelled, whereupon she divorced him because he should've said, "Are you hurt?"

Madame Kanai was *modan*. She liked Isao. They both liked to put on plays. He did backdrops and costumes for her and played bit parts in the samurai and Japanese fairy tale plays she staged for the church and the language school. Occasionally, she would put on a Western play. For their tenth-grade graduation, her students put on a ghost play called *Hamuretto,* where a son killed the uncle who had murdered his father and married his mother.

Kiyoshi couldn't keep still once he could get out of bed. He'd push himself on his haunches on the floor and play *karuta* or tag with Takako and Fumio Oshiro from next door. They would lay the sewing chair on its back and rock it from side to side and pretend it was a sampan.

"My legs hurt," he said one day.

Isao carried him to the hospital, and Mr. Kunichika X-rayed his legs. They cut off the casts. Mr. Kunichika held him under his arms while big Dr. Hall pulled one leg, then the other. They took another X ray to make sure the bones were aligned, then put on new casts.

"You have to lie still. You can't get off the bed. Otherwise, you'll end up a cripple," I said.

Isao carried him to the hospital in April to have the casts removed. The casts came off, and the reddish-brown skin peeled off his calves like a thin, rotting banana skin. Dr. Hall helped him to his feet, then let go, and Kiyoshi took his first baby-like step, then another, then another! There wasn't even a hint of a limp. "Thank you, Kami-sama," I said.

In July our fifth child was born. Aunt Kitano came down from Pepelau to help deliver her. Isao named her Miwa (three feathers).

Mrs. Woods asked the plantation to cut Kiyoshi's $700 hospital bill in half. She came to the house when Kiyoshi was absent on his first day as a second grader because he had caught a cold.

"Oh, *getto korudo; kofu-kofu,*" I coughed for her.

"Oh, I'm glad it's only a cold," she said in her soft, reedy voice.

"Sank you, sank you." I bowed and bowed.

I also felt grateful she didn't blame me for Myles Fukunaga, who was scheduled to be hanged soon. How could he not be insane? If he were sane, it'd be like saying we were all like him.

20 · The Bad Omens

The 1929 school year started out badly and got worse. First the stock market crashed, then they hanged Myles Fukunaga, then Mie-chan, our landlady, left her husband, Mr. Ando. She took her two girls and went to live with the only nisei lawyer in town, a Mr. Hirata, on Front Street. She was so vivacious and friendly, whereas her husband was a loner and a drinker. He was a nisei who'd gone to Japan for his education and now didn't seem to fit with the American-educated niseis. His Japanese was impeccable, but he spoke English like the isseis. The story was that he'd gotten Mie-chan pregnant when she was fifteen.

It fell to me to build the fire for the bath, and I kept the water hot till late for Mr. Ando. He'd always been the last to bathe, pounding in his metal shop till way past supper. But now the shop was eerily quiet. Each time I let the fire die out, I wondered if I should've knocked and asked him if he'd bathed. *It would only embarrass him,* I thought. A month later they found him hanging in his shop.

Then the house on Back Street across from the Oshiro Tailor Shop became haunted. Mr. Wei Ming, who owned the Wei Ming Clothing Store on Front Street, had bought the house from an old Kanaka family. As soon as they moved in, strange shapes and voices began to appear after midnight. An old Kanaka was buried under the house to safeguard it, and his ghost was angry, people said. Young toughs who volunteered to confront the ghost couldn't last the night.

"It's probably the wind and headlights from cars," Isao scoffed.

"What about Mr. Tanaka seeing ghosts?" He'd dismissed that too. In Kahana there'd been so many people from Fukuoka, but in Pepelau Mr. Tanaka was the only Fukuoka visitor. He was an old bachelor and a night watchman. He rode his horse to the different sluices to regulate the flow of water for the next day's irrigation. One moonless night he heard strange music and saw what looked like a moving stream of thick fog. His horse stopped abruptly and wouldn't budge. He learned later that it was the parade of dead Kanakas. They got up and marched on certain nights, and you dropped dead if you were in their path.

"How could you believe in something you can't see or touch?" Isao said.

But the Wei Mings moved out, and another house became vacant.

Soon afterward Toshio and Akira Kashima were riding a bicycle together on Front Street and were hit by a car. The wheels crushed the bicycle, but both boys crawled out from under the car with only a few scratches.

"Father, we have to move. This house is bad luck," I said.

"It's superstition," he laughed.

I kept after him. "It's also bad luck for your fishing. You haven't had a $100 day in three years!"

The omens never hit you over the head. You had to be receptive to them.

Isao finally found a house for $20 just beyond Omiya Camp. Mr. Handa, the landlord, had a small candy store on Dickensen Street next to Mr. Omiya's big dry goods store. We moved in after the New Year and right away our luck changed. I got my first order. But it was for a wedding kimono.

The nisei bride and her mother brought bolts of silk. I was so pleased I offered the bride a two-week lesson in sewing. My fee was $50, or half what professional dressmakers charged.

"Do you like this?" "How about this combination? It's so unexpected, it surprises." "Or maybe you like the traditional like this. You can never go wrong . . ." I tried one combination after another. I knew what I preferred, but satisfying them was more important. Matching was fun, but the stitching was laborious. I finished it in three months.

Then we got more good news. Chiyako got married. In another year she'd be twenty-six by Japanese age. It must've been difficult to adjust to Japanese ways after all her barefoot years in Kahana.

Where did Father Takao get the money for her dowry? I wondered. We waited and waited for the wedding photo.

"Maybe they forgot. Shall I write them?" I asked Isao.

"What if they didn't take one?"

"But it's always done," I said. Photos recorded arrivals, departures, weddings, and funerals. They were proof you were alive and prosperous.

"They would've sent one if they had it."

I thought afterward, *Poor Chiyako, there must not have been much of a dowry if they couldn't afford a handsome family portrait.* Father Takao's job at the Canadian Consulate mustn't pay much. But my mother couldn't even afford snapshots. Toru was still a ten year old in my mind and Mother a feisty forty-three. What did they look like now? Father was gone, his scowling face frozen in time.

In June I got my second order for a wedding kimono.

PART IV ✳ *1929–1935*

21 · TB

The new school year was like the New Year to the children. They came home with stories about their new teachers and classmates. Did the third graders still have to drink cod liver oil before lunch? Kiyoshi had gotten sick in second grade one afternoon after drinking a whole bottle of cod liver oil. "He's a show-off," Toshio said.

The second week of October was the Maui County fair. The teachers chaperoned the fourth-graders and up, and the plantation provided the trucks. I sewed around the clock in August and September. Toshio and Joji weren't going to be left out. Some families were so poor, their children couldn't afford the $1 circus tickets sold in the classes. I sewed them new pairs of pants and shirts, fixed them hot dogs on buns for their lunches, and gave each $1.50 spending money.

At dusk the whole town went to Liliuokalani to greet the trucks and make sure their children were on them. The children screamed and held aloft screeching toy birds, their tails spinning in the wind. They brought toys and candies for their younger siblings and talked and talked of lions and elephants and flying acrobats and clowns as tall as buildings.

Then it was Christmas. Madame Kanai and the older students lit up the big pine tree in front of the church, and every Sunday school class put on a show. We sat on the hard pews for over three hours. Every child was given his moment on stage. When it was finally over, the crowd buzzed. Heads swiveled. Suddenly Santa Claus appeared, and the children let out a deafening squeal!

But the big treat happened afterward. On exiting, everyone, including Buddhists and non-Japanese, was given a party horn and an apple, walnuts, and Christmas candies in a brown bag.

The children became a gaggle of geese, honk-honking their horns down Front Street and through the pitch-black cane field roads toward Kiawe Camp and Mill Camp.

Takako always squirreled away her nuts and candies. Kiyoshi would eat all of his, then ferret out Takako's cache.

"Kiyo-chan is stealing my candies!" she'd cry.

"You shouldn't do that," I told him, remembering Kingo's sweet tooth.

There wasn't enough money in the house for *ozoni* on my sixteenth New Year's day. I cleaned the house and cooked the fish and rice on the thirty-first to ensure a lucky year. But there was no way we could pay off $3,000. Nobody came calling and we called on nobody. Omiya Camp was only a block away, across Dickensen Street, but I missed the closeness of the old neighborhood. Mie-chan and the Kogas were gone, but I missed Mrs. Oshiro's radio bulletins. Our landlord, Mr. Handa, and his wife and two children, came to use the bathhouse, but they never socialized.

In February I got a rare letter from Ikeura. My stomach sank. No news had been good news. Now Mother said little brother Toru was dead of consumption! He'd taxed his body, working his way through junior college. "What are you going to do about it?" she wrote.

Why didn't she ask older sister Tomi, who had five boys? I wasn't about to give up one of mine.

We sent her $25 we borrowed from Tani Fish Market. I wrote the ritual words of sympathy but ignored her question.

In March Isao had to bring up his boat to scrape off the barnacles and repaint it—all the things I didn't know about fishing. There was absolutely no income except from my sewing. He more often than not lost money when he went out, but at least he was working. The days of making extra money from sumo and painting backdrops were *pau*. The sumo wrestlers and theater troupes stopped coming after the 1929 stock market crash.

"Children are the poor man's treasure," the proverb says. It should add, "The treasure is why he's so poor." Kiyoshi was so skinny that his teacher, Miss Hida, wanted him to drink milk at recess. It would cost another 5 cents. Some days there wasn't a penny in the house. We couldn't afford the school lunches, which also cost

5 cents. I'd cook rice every morning and fill the rectangular aluminum lunch boxes. The teachers inspected the lunches for vegetables, so I'd lay a leaf of head lettuce on the bed of rice.

"I feel *hila hila* every time I have to open my lunch," Toshio kept saying.

Then they gave a skin test at school. The insides of the children's forearms swelled up like boils. I was in a panic! Azumi, Isao's younger brother, had just contracted TB and was in Leahi Home in Honolulu. Uncle Jukichi's son had died of it back home. It ran in the family! What if all four children were sent to Kula? People who went there for TB were seldom seen again. "Please, Kami-sama," I prayed, "I didn't mean to make a joke about children causing poverty."

Just recently a young nisei had died of TB. Seizen Kudaka came from a poor family of eight boys in Kiawe Camp. Being the oldest, he had gone to work after grade school as a brakeman, running and guiding the cane cars down the slopes. He was a star in the plantation-sponsored football, basketball, and soccer games, and a champion boxer. One day he collapsed at work and died. His lungs were gone.

"What's going to happen?" I asked Toshio.

"They're taking X rays," he said.

"When?"

"I don't know. There're quite a few with three-plus—all Japanese."

"They'll send you to Kula if the X rays are bad?"

"I guess so."

I could hardly wait for the children to come home. "Did you take your X-ray?" I asked each time.

Then one day Takako said yes, they all walked to the plantation hospital and took X rays.

"*Doh? . . .*" I asked Toshio.

"*Shiran,*" he said. "They'll come to the house if our lungs are infected."

A week later an older nisei woman with a pageboy and a blue and white nurse's uniform came to the house. My heart beat so hard my whole body shook. *Please, Kami-sama . . .*

She introduced herself. "I'm Miss Wada, the public health nurse." She flipped through some papers on her clipboard. "I see you've been to Kula."

"But that was for exhaustion. We were in the nontubercular cottages."

"All your children are susceptible to tuberculosis."

"They have to go to Kula?"

"No, their X rays were negative . . ."

"Thank you."

"But Kiyoshi is 20 percent underweight. He can't lose any more weight. If he does, he'll contract tuberculosis."

"He's such a finicky eater. He won't eat but one bowl of rice. I scold him, 'One bowl is what we put out for the dead!' Miss Hida has him drink milk at recess. He's so active, he can't sit still," I said.

"Toshio is so small for his age," she said.

"He hates fish, so I buy canned corned beef and make him patties."

"Can they take school lunch?"

It'd be 50 cents more a week. I had trouble raising the weekly 25 cents for Kiyoshi's milk.

"I cook them all the rice and fish they can eat."

"What about just for Kiyoshi?"

"Yes," I said, wondering how I was going to raise another 25 cents. I explained to Toshio, Joji, and Takako why Kiyoshi had to have school lunch.

The boys were so active they'd bolt from the table while still chewing their food. Joji was easygoing like his father, but Kiyoshi already slouched. "Stand up straight!" I kept tellling him, remembering Uncle Taniguchi.

A couple of days later Toshio came home fuming. "That old maid Wada is picking on us because you went to Kula."

She had come into the classroom and examined Toshio's lunch. His classmates had looked at him as if he had TB.

"I hope you didn't tell her about Honolulu uncle."

"No."

"You must've. Why else would she single me out?"

"She must have records."

Why is she so meddlesome? I thought. *Yakunin kusai.* Stinking of bureaucrats. I started each time I thought I spied her blue and white uniform.

Just after we got over the TB scare, Liliuokalani had a dental inspection. All three boys had several cavities each. Takako, who still had some baby teeth, had only one cavity. Speaking of the "stink of

124

bureaucrats"—the children had to inform their teachers of their follow-up dental work. What business was it of theirs? I sent them one by one, beginning with Toshio, to Dr. Hamaguchi.

Just after Kiyoshi had his three cavities filled, Toshio came home from Liliuokalani with a swollen lip and his two front teeth missing!

"I beat up Masaki Kinoshita!" he bragged.

"But he knocked out your teeth!"

"But I gave him two black eyes!"

"You call that winning? I'll have Father talk to Masaki-san's father."

"No! No! I won!"

"I'd rather you'd got the black eyes instead."

"But he cried and quit. I won!"

"Ah, so?" I said. His *kapakahi* retorts always stumped me.

He looked so silly covering his mouth. At least it slowed down his back talk.

Soon after the school's dental inspection, a *haole*-Japanese *hapa*, Dr. Tester, opened an office in Hop Kee Camp on Back Street. He rented one of the identical green and white frame houses in which the Filipino bachelors lived. People said he charged half the price of Dr. Hamaguchi. *He's half Japanese so he must be honorable,* I thought. Besides, I didn't want to run up the bills at Dr. Hamaguchi's.

Dr. Tester asked for $40 in advance. He looked more *haole* than Japanese. He was a big, fat man with a double chin, and he waddled when he walked. I *oppa*ed Miwa and went with Toshio and sat in the waiting room, which had been the parlor. The office was the former bedroom.

"You have to *gaman*," I told Toshio.

"You don't have to come," Toshio said on his next visit.

It took four visits to get his bridge installed. I was able to finish the kimono in time to send Toshio with the second half of the payment.

That night Toshio's face swelled up.

"It hurts," he said.

The next morning we hurried to the Filipino camp. The house looked strangely quiet. Mrs. Sakai and her daughter were on the veranda, peering through the windows.

"What's happened?" I asked, and peered in.

The single couch and two chairs were gone from the "waiting

room." I could see only part of the "office," but the dental chair and grinding machine were gone.

"He's run away. He took our money and ran away," Mrs. Sakai said. "He collected money in advance from a dozen people."

Dr. Hamaguchi said the next two teeth were infected and had to be pulled. The extractions and new bridge cost $120.

"That's what you get for acting *piitare*," Toshio sneered.

"It's all my fault; forgive me," I said. "I thought he must be honorable, being half Japanese. It must be the *haole* half that's crooked."

I could smell the rot in my mouth, but my teeth could wait.

22 · The Depression

The boys practically lived in the ocean during summer. Joji and Kiyoshi went spearfishing every day. On Sundays Sadao Ono, Aunt Kitano's son, would drive them past Honolua and they'd bring home half a barley bag of green-and-black striped *manini,* which were tastier than Isao's fish.

"There were so many, Joji and Kiyoshi would spear them and fling them onto the beach," Sadao said.

"Even Kiyo speared over two dozen!" Joji said.

Joji took Kiyoshi everywhere he went, whereas Toshio played only with Kanakas, Filipinos, and Chinese.

"Did Papa go out today?" Toshio asked one day.

"No." I sat on a cushion on the floor, sewing a kimono. I was also getting orders for pants and shirts.

"Where is he?"

"I don't know. At the wharf or Tani Fish Market."

"You know, Father is on the lazy side."

"Don't you dare bad-mouth your father," I said.

"Mr. Masuda, whenever he can't go out, slings his lunch bag over his shoulder and goes to work at the pineapple cannery."

"So?"

"I'm just telling you what I see. Mr. Masuda works at the cannery when he can't fish. Why doesn't Papa do that?"

"Mr. Masuda isn't the fisherman your father is. He can't even stay out overnight."

"I still think Papa is on the lazy side. He likes to drink and talk story."

"Why can't you show him some respect?"

"He shows *me* no respect."

"What do you mean?"

"Whenever I swim up to his skiff, he pushes me off. Then he lets the Filipino and Kanaka boys on and lets them take the oar. They all laugh at me! My own father treats me like dirt!"

"You must've said something."

"All I do is look inside his bags. It's all *paka* nowadays. *Onaga* is *pau*. You know, I think Tani is a crook. He invites Papa for a beer in the back while his wife weighs the catch. It happens every time. She subtracts ten to fifteen pounds."

"How do you know?"

"Satsuma, the insurance salesman, told me. He ought to know. He hangs around town all day. He told me, 'Check it out, I think they cheating your father.' And so I checked, and sure enough, Mrs. Tani knocked off ten pounds. Not only once, but three times. You should talk to him and tell him not to drink beer till after he weighs the catch."

"Your father is too honest."

"Not honest; dumb."

"They call him the *onaga* king."

"So when's the last time he caught *onaga?*"

"You act like you know everything."

"Not everything; just what I see. Nobody's catching anything."

He walked out.

It was true. Fishing was bad. Tani and the other fish markets refused the mahimahis Isao caught trolling. He would bring them home and give pieces to the Oshiros, Katos, and others. The children called it "throwaway fish." The $100 days were long *pau*. He'd fished out Mr. Baker's fishing grounds and kept going farther and farther out.

"Maybe we should think of returning to Kahana," I said.

"I'll be throwing away all my knowledge of the sea. I'm a good fisherman; I take risks. I need a bigger boat. I need to find new fishing grounds."

"Or we could go to another camp."

"I can't go back to irrigating cane."

"Maybe you can get your engineer's job back in Mr. Kawai's steam plow gang."

"Steam plow is *pau*. They have tractors now."

"He'll give you a job in his tractor gang, then. He owes us."

Just when things are so bleak, something happens that makes you realize your troubles are trivial. Mrs. Kato ran away from her family in Omiya Camp and went to live with Mr. Shimazu, the barber, on Dickensen Street, only half a block away. What outraged people was that she sat on the bench outside the barbershop every afternoon.

"How could she flaunt her shame?" everybody said. You expected behavior like that from a nisei, maybe.

We wouldn't have been involved except that Mitsunobu Kato was Kiyoshi's best friend and we'd given them pieces of mahimahi. Mitsunobu told his father, "Don't worry, Father, Kiyoshi and I will link arms and go to college together. We're the best students in our class." He was the baby of the family. His brother and four sisters were adults.

Mr. Kato worked for Mr. Robinson on the plantation. The "Robinson gang" dynamited rocks and cleared fields, and they were paid well. People said Mr. Kato drank a lot and beat his wife, but Isao said he was a man "who knew his obligations." The barber, Mr. Shimazu, was an old widower with two married daughters. He was a short man with curly hair and a Charlie Chaplin mustache. Mrs. Kato was no great beauty, either. People had thought nothing of it when she'd spent whole afternoons sitting on the bench outside the barbershop. Now she was like an open sore.

Then it was the new school year and a big scandal rocked Honolulu. Five boys, including one Japanese, raped the *haole* wife of an American navy officer. Isao came home from sea and told me about it. Now I broke open the paper seals and scanned the three-day-old news. It wasn't as shameful as the Fukunaga case. It wasn't murder, and the nisei was only one of five, but it still made me cringe.

A few issues later the bold headlines said the Japanese army attacked the Chinese in Mukden for blowing up the Manchurian railway.

"Is there going to be war?" I asked Isao.

"No, it's just an incident."

I felt relieved when the jury couldn't decide if the five boys were guilty. Maybe they'd arrested the wrong people. Soon afterward some white sailors kidnapped the nisei and beat him up to try to get a confession.

We celebrated my seventeenth New Year's day with only *paka* cooked whole. It was a relief nobody called on us. Back in Kahana we had pounded *mochi* together and celebrated as a community. We were all poor. Isao's *Hyotan-kai,* the club of successful entrepreneurs, had not met since 1929. "The depression is worldwide," people said. The countries had put up tariff barriers and dried up trade. The bad luck was worldwide. Running a block away was futile.

Soon after the mistrial, the rape story took a more scandalous turn. The husband and mother of the raped woman kidnapped the Kanaka and murdered him and were caught trying to dispose of the body.

Then, before the month was over, the Chinese in Shanghai killed a Japanese Buddhist priest and attacked other Japanese. The Japanese landed troops, touching off the "Shanghai Incident."

The Mukden and Shanghai incidents dragged on. One day the paper carried a headline about the *Bakudan San-yuhshi.* Three soldiers carried a torpedo-like bomb into a Chinese barbed wire barricade in Shanghai and blew themselves up so that their comrades could charge through the opening.

"Do they have to go to such extremes?" I asked.

"It's the Japanese spirit," Isao said.

Then Manchuria became Manchukuo, a Japanese protectorate.

"Japan needs a forward base in her coming war against Russia," Isao explained.

"Why must there be war?"

"The communists plan to conquer China."

It was going to be a bad year. My molars hurt so much I had to chew my food with my front teeth.

"We have to return to the plantation," I kept nagging.

"You're asking me to give up my feudal domain to become a slave."

"But you're not earning a living as a feudal lord."

One day Kiyoshi and Mitsunobu were walking home from Liliuo-kalani when Mitsunobu spotted his mother on the bench. "Let's go the other way. She my mother but I no can stand her," he said. When Kiyoshi looked back, she'd stood up with arms extended. It was so sad.

"Isn't it pitiful?" I said at supper.

"How can you deal with somebody who knows no shame?" Isao said.

"Heh-heh," Toshio said. "*Obaban* did the same thing, didn't she?"

"*Bakatare!*" Isao yelled.

"*Obaban's* case was different. Her first husband left for Japan with the children," I said.

"What's so different?" Toshio sneered.

"It allowed *Obaban* to get on with her life."

"As if nothing happened?"

"Mrs. Kato is an open embarrassment. She'd be shunned if she lived in Kahana," Isao said.

"She's shunned now," Toshio said.

"But only in Omiya Camp," I replied.

"Shunning is shunning."

But what Father is saying is it'd be different in Kahana! I was going to say, but stopped. It'd be like arguing with Mother Haru.

One had to leave shame behind and start life anew. Even with Myles Fukunaga's parents. The community had raised enough money to return them to Japan.

✳ ✳ ✳

A month later Mr. Shimazu and Mrs. Kato left for Japan. So that's why she went to him. He'd promised to take her back to Japan. She must've been really homesick, people said.

"Do people get that homesick?" Kiyoshi asked one day.

"Hmmm . . ."

"Would you?"

"One shouldn't think of one's personal happiness. Obligations come first," I said.

In March there was a national scandal. Somebody kidnapped Charles Lindbergh's baby. *I hope he doesn't kill the child like Fukunaga,* I prayed. The world was being turned upside down. I followed the Honolulu murder trial halfheartedly. They were just going through the motions. Nobles and samurais can kill peasants, but not vice versa. Sure enough, the navy officer and his mother-in-law were found guilty and sentenced to ten years, but their sentences were commuted to one hour.

"There's a law for whites and a separate law for nonwhites," Isao huffed.

"The crime was not knowing one's place. One should never cross the line," I said.

"It's insulting to be treated as an inferior! Like all the unequal treaties the white nations imposed on Japan! You just can't sit and take it!" he said.

When school ended, we got another shock. Joji failed fifth grade. Isao took him to school to see his teacher. Mrs. Behr explained that Joji was absent half the time. Isao pleaded, please let Joji pass; he'd see to it personally that Joji attended every class next year.

Joji was so healthy and undemanding that he got lost between Toshio and Kiyoshi. While playing marbles as a child, he'd get so involved that, rather than take time to urinate, he'd squeeze his penis and continue to play.

He had gone fishing. He'd come home about two o'clock, then leave for language school. If he'd cut language school, Madame Kanai would've inquired if he was sick. A nisei teacher at Liliuokalani would've done the same. Except for Mrs. Woods, the *haole* teachers didn't seem to care. It was what freedom amounted to—not caring.

Isao brought out his calligraphy box and wrote on old newspapers, "*Benkyo wa kohfuku no haha nari*"

勉強は幸福の母なり

"Study is the mother of good fortune." He had Joji copy the proverb over and over. The irony was that Joji had the best hand of all the children. He'd won several awards for his calligraphy at language school. He'd even won a territorial prize for a drawing of *Nasu-no-Yoichi* in the battle of Yashima. Isao also had Takako copy the same proverb in the hopes of raising her grades.

"A girl being a C student is all right," I said.

Girls needed to know only how to sew and cook and not get pregnant till marriage. The worst thing was to get pregnant by a *haole*, Kanaka, Chinese, Filipino, or Portuguese. There was a story of a mother on the other side of the island. She drank a whole bottle of soy sauce and faked suicide to keep her daughter from marrying a Chinese. But I didn't have to worry about Takako for the time being.

Mother wrote from Ikeura with some rare good news. Older sister Tomi agreed to give up her third son to her. There was nothing to inherit, but he'd keep the Ito family tree from dying out.

The good news was followed by bad news from Tokyo. Kingo was dead! He'd ruined his health working his way through business school. Father Takao had written earlier, "His English is so good, he's in great demand, teaching and giving talks, and he's had offers from several companies." A month after graduation he was dead of TB. We borrowed another $25, this time from Aoki Nobuo, to send as "incense offering." I felt bad that I had not told Kingo I held no grudge about his stealing. He was so young; he must've thought the money belonged to everybody. He must've really craved the creamy chocolate bars. By contrast, Japanese candies were so dry and barely sweet. But it had hurt so much I couldn't talk about it. Besides, it would've embarrassed him if I'd brought it up. It saved his face if I pretended it hadn't happened.

23 · What Did We Do Wrong?

I dreaded the first of the month when I had to ask for another extension on the rent.

I kept after Isao. "We have to go back to the plantation."

The plantation kept hiring despite the depression.

"Our debt is now $3,500! Doesn't that worry you?"

I suggested his working at the pineapple cannery on days he couldn't fish. They weren't hiring; pineapples were being left to rot in the fields, he said.

Aoki Nobuo, the fourteen year old who had boarded with us in 1921, now owned a prosperous grocery store on Front Street. We bought all our food and dry goods from him. He let us charge as much as we wanted, and he didn't come to collect every month like the others.

What if we asked Mr. Aoki to let Toshio work part-time at his store? I thought. Liliuokalani School let out at 1:30 P.M., so he could work there all afternoon and into the night. We could apply half of his pay to what we owed the store. I discussed it with Isao and Toshio, and Isao spoke to Mr. Aoki, who said he would pay Toshio 30 cents to work from 3:00 to 9:00 P.M. on weekdays, 60 cents for twelve hours on Saturdays, and 30 cents for half days on Sundays. He'd earn about $10 a month and bring home about $5. Toshio would have to quit language school, of course, which was too bad. *Where else would he learn discipline?* I thought.

"We're so poor we have to borrow your body," I explained.

"It's Papa's fault," he said. "He should quit fishing."

"Father'll talk to Reverend Kanai when he comes home today."

"I'll tell him," he said, leaving for his first day of work.

The store closes at 9:00, so he'll be home around 9:15, and I'll fix him his favorite dish of fried potatoes if he's hungry, I was thinking, when he came storming into the house without washing his feet.

"Kanai hit me! He hit me in front of the whole class!" he yelled.

"Why?"

"I just told him I was quitting school!"

"You must've said something," I said. You never knew what'd come out of his mouth.

"All I said was I was quitting school! He hit my head and kept hitting me in front of the whole class!"

"It's my fault. I should've talked to him first. Come, let's go apologize," Isao said.

"Apologize?! Apologize?! He hits me and you want me to apologize? You Japanese are so *kapakahi!*"

Isao went by himself to apologize.

I thought about it afterward. He'd been hit in the afternoon. Then he went directly to work. The anger had been boiling in him for six hours! What a strange boy!

A couple of months later Toshio came home to bathe before going back to the store. It was on a Saturday, when he worked all day. Takako was in the bathhouse.

"Hey, Taka, hurry up! I gotta go back to work!" he yelled.

When Takako didn't come out, Toshio went in and grabbed her hand and pulled her out. She screamed. She was stark naked, her hair soaped.

Isao, who was cleaning fish at the outside sink, kicked off his *geta* and swung it at Toshio's head. *"Chikusho!"*

Toshio released Takako, who ran back into the bathhouse.

Toshio rubbed his head and looked at his palm. "I'm going to be late for work."

"Are you hurt?" I rushed up to him.

"You hit me! Kanai hit me! Next time I goin' hit back!"

It really upset me. What did we do wrong? Were the *kyokai* teachers too soft? You never heard of students talking back to the priests at the Buddhist schools. They'd be pounded down like protruding nails. Then I realized it was bigger than the Buddhist or Christian schools. The language schools had them for only an hour a day. How could you teach discipline in one short hour? It was no wonder the rich families sent their children to Japan for their education. Education meant discipline.

Father Takao wrote from Tokyo, ". . . She lost her will to live after Kingo died." Mother Haru was dead at sixty-three. *It must run in the family,* I thought. My own father had also quit. I'd been on my way to Kula at that time and didn't have the strength to grieve. Now I felt only anger. After he'd gambled away what was left of the family farm, he quit. He didn't care what happened to Mother and Toru.

A week later the younger Mrs. Kuni stopped at the house after school to offer *koden,* or incense money, for Mother Haru. The older Mrs. Kuni, the widow, still had her candy store in Kahana. She'd sent her son to the normal school in Honolulu, and now Robert Kuni was a teacher at Kahana Grade School and his wife was Kiyoshi's teacher at Liliuokalani.

"You know, Kiyoshi is such a good student I could jump him into the next grade. He'll have no trouble," she said.

"*Mah, mah* . . ." I said, surprised and pleased. "But he's so skinny. He can't keep still."

"Maybe it's because he's bored."

"I'll talk to Father," I said, and thanked her.

I had no trouble convincing Isao. Kiyoshi's health was more important. But the main reason was Joji. If Joji had to compete with Kiyoshi, he would quit. He was so easygoing while Kiyoshi was all nerves. Ever since Kiyoshi was run over by the car, Joji looked after him like a second parent. They looked so alike people couldn't tell them apart. Even I would call Joji Kiyoshi and vice versa and would often mistake their voices. Never once had Joji sent Kiyoshi home crying from the playgrounds as Toshio had done so often with Joji.

I ran a fever on the day of Toshio's graduation. My toothaches now inflamed my whole mouth. Isao had gone to sea, thinking I'd attend. I couldn't get up. I thought of sending Joji with a lei, but I didn't even have money for one.

Several days later Toshio brought home the photo of his graduation class. He was the runt of the class! You saw only the top of his face peeping from behind the shoulders of his classmates! Why didn't they put him up front? Did his classmates bully him? Was that why he was so obsessed with boxing?

✳ ✳ ✳

"The Three Human Bombs," *Bakudan San-yuhshi,* came to the Nippon Theater. The movie dealt with the three brave soldiers who carried the bomb into the barricades in Shanghai in 1932. I gave the children 10 cents each to go see it. Toshio took the money but refused to go.

"I have some Chinese friends," he said. "Besides, the Japanese lie. They kill the Chinese and tell them it's to save them from communism."

"But they are fighting the communists," I said.

"Chiang Kai Shek is not a communist! The students are not communists! The League of Nations is not communist!"

I felt so weak I shut up. But why was he so angry all the time?

I felt as rundown as I did in 1921. Except now my body was twelve years older and my teeth ached and stank. I'd get up to sew and the sky would darken and I'd crawl back to the futon in the bedroom. *But I have to get up,* I kept telling myself. Toshio needed street shoes for high school. His feet had spread so much he needed shoes two sizes larger. He refused to take his rice lunch in the rectangular lunch boxes. I made patties from canned corned beef, using lots of potato to make the corned beef last.

✳ ✳ ✳

Mr. Yamanoha, who had a piggery in Pump Camp, paid 10 cents for a barley bag of *kiawe* beans, which the pigs loved. The beans fell during the night from the trees in the kindergarten and other parts of town. Whoever got up first picked them clean. The Tanimura brothers from Omiya Camp got up at 5:30 A.M., so I woke Joji and Kiyoshi at 5:00. When they got up at 4:30, I woke my boys at 4:00, after which the Tanimura boys gave up. I might have one foot in the grave, but we weren't going to lose to anybody.

Every letter from Tokyo was bad news. Chiyako divorced her husband and took her child to live with Father Takao and Masako. It must be difficult adjusting to Japanese ways after growing up here. *Can Father Takao support them on his pay at the Canadian Consulate?* I wondered. He hadn't asked for more money. My own mother was even more indigent, working as a maid at an elementary school for her room and board.

24 · Dying in a Strange Land

I could no longer chew. My teeth wobbled.

"Your gums are infected. They all have to come out," Dr. Hamaguchi said. "They're loose, so pulling them won't be difficult." He advised pulling the lowers one week and the uppers the next. Was it cheaper pulling them all today? I asked. He said it would be $2 less.

"Please pull them all today," I begged.

He injected Novocain into the backs of my lower gums, stuffed rolls of cotton beside them, and pulled out one tooth after another. The rolls of cotton dripped with blood.

"Would you like to stop?" he asked, after he'd pulled all the lowers.

"No," I gurgled. I needed to *gaman* only a few more minutes to save $2.

Then he injected the corners of the upper gums, and the numbness spread to my cheekbones.

The uppers also came out easily, but now the blood gushed.

"There," he said finally.

Just then my eyeballs rolled back and the lights went out.

❋   ❋   ❋

I gag and cough, looking for somewhere to spit. A cup nearby is filled with blood.

Where am I? I hear my strange voice say.

138

You're at my hospital. Dr. Kawamura peers at me behind his thick glasses.

I raise my head and the room spins and everything goes dark again.

It's pitch black when I wake up. Am I dead? I float up to the ceiling.

Kokua shite! Help me! Pull! I yell but I have no voice.

Then I'm playing tag with Toru, and Mother and Father are laughing.

When I awake, it's daylight and I'm back in bed. My mouth is swollen; my gums throb. There's nobody else in the three-bed hospital.

❉　❉　❉

Then the bleeding stops and the pain returns. They take me home. I crawl out to the parlor and fight against the dizziness. I promised the kimono for the wedding.

"Why don't you sew something easy like pants or a dress?" Kiyoshi says.

"There's more money in a kimono."

"Why don't you sit on a chair or at the sewing machine where you can stretch your legs?"

"There's a proper way of doing everything."

But I get dizzy again and crawl back to the futon on the bedroom floor.

"Mother, Mother," a little girl's voice keeps calling. Oh, it's little Miwa, who's been assigned to baby-sit me.

"Mother, Mother? Oh, I think she's sleeping. Yeah, I can go," she says.

I hear steps leaving the veranda, the happy voices of her playmates. I remember scolding Takako, "You can't go out to play until you finish your sewing lesson!"

I feel guilty not having paid enough attention to Miwa. I never took her to the wharf or the playground at the kindergarten or played *karuta* with her. But she never acted up.

I get up and comb my disheveled hair and go back to my sewing.

Then it happens again.

❉　❉　❉

When I awake, an oval face, a filigree of hair, hovers. Am I dead? *Oyama-san?*

Hai—bowing upward to the angelic face.

The doctor says you're suffering from exhaustion and loss of blood. Otherwise, you're all right. You have no fever. So gambatte, ne? You can't lose. You have to get well, ne?

I'm sorry to be such a nuisance.

You're not a nuisance.

I'm so worthless.

You're not worthless. You're remarkable.

I wanted to borrow some of her flowing flapper dresses. They're simpler than kimonos, and I can charge more. But only she and the *haoles* wore them.

You have to want *to get well, ne? It'd be mortifying to die in a strange land.*

I'm sorry to be such trouble.

You're no trouble.

Was Madame Kanai really here? Or was it another dream? *Dying in a strange land.* It must've been her. Being childless, she has nobody to care for her if she dies here. It must worry her.

I hadn't fainted since I was a little child. I remember the terror of those little deaths. What if I don't wake up the next time? What if I wake up in a world of strangers?

✳ ✳ ✳

They take me home again. I crawl out to the parlor.

"I'll tell them you can't do it! I'll ask them to give it to Nakai!" Isao yanks away the kimono.

"But I promised it for the wedding. Besides, they can't afford what a professional charges."

"You don't have the strength."

"But the rent is due."

"I've asked him for another extension!"

Please don't scold me; I need to be pampered. I can't sit up, anyway. The floor tilts and my head spins. Isao stays home and cooks and launders. He spoon-feeds me rice gruel and crushed fish. But the smell nauseates.

"*Gambatte, gambatte,*" he says.

Why do we keep exhorting each other to persevere? We must lack stamina. My own father quit, then Mother Haru, and little brothers Toru and Kingo. No, the boys didn't quit. They pushed themselves till their bodies crumbled. They must've skimped on food and rest. *Yamato damashi* said the Japanese were special; we didn't need food or rest. Our spirit could overcome TB; even rotten teeth.

Isao says, "Don't worry; you worry too much. That's why you get sick."

"I wouldn't if you did!" I yell, and am startled awake. It irritated me the way he brushed off everything with a flick of the wrist.

It's so boring to be caged in a sick body. If only I could sleep; if I could soap off this sticky film of sweat and wake up cool and squeaky-clean. I miss the big *ohai* tree. Here the naked sun beats down on the roof and bakes the room. In Japan, no matter how sultry, October had always brought a respite. The skies turned brilliant, and chestnuts, grapes, and persimmons ripened, and the maple leaves turned crimson. I'd like so much to see it all once more.

Dr. Kawamura brings more pills and bottles.

I grimace. "They're not working."

"You need food more than medicines," he says.

"And rest. I wish I could go back to Kula." Talking contorts my face.

"You need to get fitted for dentures."

But I don't want to throw away money on a corpse! I think.

I don't feel dizzy the next time I get up. I go to the Singer and work on trousers. I get 50 cents a pair and I can knock one off in two hours. But I shake so much I have to lie down. My heart feels so tired. How can the body be so wasted and the mind so clear?

Oh, for a breath of winter chill! Deep winter, snow, and frozen toes. Unheated classrooms and hardship strengthened you. Numb fingers in calligraphy class, writing over and over: *Raku wa ku no tane, ku wa raku no tane*

樂は苦の種、苦は樂の種

"Luxury begets suffering, and suffering luxury."

Each proverb was illustrated with a story. When Confucius was a little boy, he lived next to fishmongers. All day long he imitated them, hawking fish. "We can't have this," his mother said, and moved the family next to a temple. He spent his days chanting like the bonzes. Finally his mother moved the family next to a college. Confucius imitated the scholars and grew up to become a great sage.

We have to move back to Kahana. They still celebrated the emperor's birthday there. Pepelau has too many *gaijins*, and the Japanese are scattered. Shame no longer works.

Mr. Omiya ran a monthly card game in his home behind the store. He hired Mrs. Morita from across town to pour *sake* for the gamblers. People had seen her, weaving her way home on Front Street early in the morning in her kimono and powdered face. "Doesn't Mr. Morita make enough on his salesman's commission? . . . A beautiful wife is a drawback," people said.

Mr. Yamashita on Front Street also had a beautiful wife. The bachelors went to his tailor shop just to gawk, and one of them, a rich fabric salesman, became a boarder. He was in love with Mrs. Yamashita, people whispered, and he supplied Mr. Yamashita with *sake* and much more. How else could Mr. Yamashita have sent all his children to high school and the boys on to college?

It was no wonder the boys were losing their manners. They've stopped saying, *"Gochiso sama!"*, *"Tada-ima!"*, and all the rituals of good manners. Rituals inculcated manners, and manners were morals. What would Confucius' mother have done?

It's another lie. Suffering does not beget luxury. When was our luxury? The three short years when Isao was *onaga* king? No, suffering begets more suffering, and death, death. Like Toru, like Kingo. Poor boys; they never had a chance. They were pushed by their mothers to succeed where their fathers had failed. Poor Mother Haru—marrying Father Takao only begat suffering. It happened in cycles of fours. *Shi* 死 "death" is *shi* 四 "four." I'm the fourth.

My comb falls out, and I pick it up without stepping on it first. Picking up a "comb," *kushi,* means also picking up the other *kushi,* or "painful death."

Isao yells, "I'm sick of all your puns. *Shi-shi* is also 'piss'!"

"I'm so worthless; I hope you think well of me after . . ." I *amaeru* to the children.

"Mama, don't worry about the debt. I'll be able to work full time in a few years. I'll help," Toshio says.

"Thank you so much." I bow upward, tears streaming down my temples. "Joji and Kiyoshi will help too, but I need to borrow your body most of all . . ." I cry so easily now. I'll be so happy if this makes him filial again, the way he was before I went to Kula.

"Why me? Why me?" I keep asking. "I must be chosen for somebody else's *bachi*."

"*Bakatare. Bachi* is superstition. Some bad luck is bound to happen to anybody if he waits long enough," Isao says quietly.

Kiyoshi is the only one who lets me *amaeru*. He understands we need to be pampered. He's been near death, too.

"We've never done anything that bad," he says.

"No, but a close relative might have. We can get punished as the substitute."

If only I could go back to Kula. I'll even force myself to eat the foul-smelling cheese. Their foods were so nutritious, I felt myself growing stronger day by day. Maybe that's why we keep exhorting, "Persevere, persevere." We lack the right foods. So we call on our spirit to make up for our poverty and poor diet. Dr. Hall, Dr. Sherwood, or Miss Wada could have saved Toru and Kingo. "Meddlesome bureaucrats" they were not. But then maybe only rich governments could afford to give free skin tests and X rays and dental inspections.

Mrs. Kato, now Mrs. Shimazu, returns from Japan and sits outside the barbershop, but her troubles no longer lessen my pain. It's so easy to just lie here and not get up. Mr. Noda, who worked at the pump station in Honokawai below Kahana, got a ride after work. He stood on the running board and an oncoming car hit him and killed him instantly. The eldest boy had to quit high school and go to work in the cane fields to support the family. Right in Omiya Camp, Mr. Kosaka, a bonito fisherman, died of a heart attack. Tet-chan, who'd graduated with Toshio, took a job at the mill, 6:00 P.M. to 6:00 A.M. He looked ghostly pale from all the nightwork. Back in Kahana, Reverend Morimoto died of the Spanish flu, leaving Madame Morimoto with three girls. And there was Mr. Shinagawa, who picked at the sore in his nose and died at age thirty-six. His widow now worked with the women's gang, weeding and cutting cane seedlings. "Earthquake, thunder, fire, and father," they say in Japan, but the terror in Hawaii is to be left a widow with a houseful of children. But what if the wife died first? What will the children remember of me?

I tell Kiyoshi, "It's too bad you're not the number one son. You're wiser than Toshio and not a *kolohe* boy like Joji. See to it that Toshio and Father don't fight so much . . ."

I think about it afterward. *Why is Father so hard on Toshio? Why can't he treat him the way he treats Joji and Kiyoshi?* He takes Joji and Kiyoshi and their classmates out on his boat for a day of fishing. He takes them out again even if they got seasick the first time and begged him to take them back. *He's only wasting money on gas and bait,* I kept thinking, but he enjoyed entertaining the boys. Why can't he do the same for Toshio? Is that why Toshio hates fish so?

I tell Joji and Kiyoshi that we are Mr. Aoki's benefactor, so he'll keep extending us credit. "But we owe Tani Fish Market $1,000, the dentist . . . Dr. Kawamura . . . they're all in the ledger in the sewing machine drawer. Except for Mr. Aoki and Tani, you have to pay them at least $2 a month to show them you're sincere."

"Rest. Take care of the body," Joji said. "Toshio, Kiyoshi, and me, we'll be working in no time, and we'll pay off the debt."

"Thank you, thank you."

✳ ✳ ✳

The heat is so oppressive. If I could only take off my flesh and lie down in my bones. What am I saying? I feel trapped, like Mrs. Kato (I keep calling her Mrs. Kato). "Why doesn't she leave?" people say. But how can she when *he* does not? It's Mr. Shimazu who doesn't know shame. It can't be helped. We're only women. We *gaman* too much, they pile too much on us; it's a Japanese disease.

✳ ✳ ✳

"Oh, where's Father?" I woke one morning to find him gone.

"He went out to sea yesterday," Kiyoshi says.

"Why aren't you at school?"

"I thought I'd stay home."

"Is it all right?"

"I can catch up easily."

"You know, *Obaban* hasn't come to see me," I sigh. Sadao-san hasn't visited in months either. He's probably made new friends.

"Shall I go get her?"

"It costs too much to hire a taxi."

144

"I can phone the plantation store from Aoki Store and ask her to come. She doesn't know you're sick."

"I don't want to trouble her."

"I'll go get her," he says.

"*Sumimasen.*" I bow and drift off into half-sleep.

✳   ✳   ✳

When I open my eyes, *Obaban*'s fullness is at the doorway.

"Kitano-san?"

"Sawa-chan."

I sit up and we hold each other.

"I had to see you before I die!"

"You're not going to die."

"I can feel it."

"Your karma is decided the moment you're born. Your time is not now." Her voice is soft and deep.

"How do you know?"

"I know."

"What if I'm being chosen as a substitute for someone else's *bachi?*"

"Find another substitute," she laughs, "and you'll be spared."

"You know, I borrowed a handful of dirt from the San-O shrine when I came to Hawaii. I promised I'd return it without fail in five years. Could you return—" I catch myself. So stupid!

"You'll return it," she chuckles. "You'll go back for a visit some day. But life is better here. You're more free to be yourself. As hard as plantation life is, I think life in Japan is harder. We're often nostalgic for something that never existed."

"*Ah, so? . . .*"

"But first you must come back to Kahana. You have to tell your master. In a year he'll have been a fisherman for fifteen years. If he hasn't succeeded by then, he should give it up and return to the plantation . . ."

"Oh, thank you so much. I'm so worthless . . ."

"You're remarkable. People still talk about you in Kahana."

"But I'm so useless . . ."

"You get sick because you work too hard. Try to be lazy and really useless like the others," she laughs.

I feel light-headed afterward and drift off into a deep sleep. I dream Toru is just born and Father is so delighted he dances, cradling him. It stays with me. It was a happy time. But Mother and older sister Tomi were not in the dream! It was the dead beckoning me!

"I'm so relieved. I wanted to see Aunt Kitano one last time," I say to Isao when he comes home from sea.

"*Bakatare*," he says softly. "You'll outlive us all."

The next morning Mr. Tanji, the delivery man for Aoki Store, drives his pickup to the house in a cloud of dust. There was a phone call from the plantation store in Kahana. Aunt Kitano had suffered a stroke.

"But she was so healthy yesterday!"

"She wasn't feeling well this morning, so Mr. Kitano stayed home from work. She collapsed later," Mr. Tanji says.

Isao goes ahead.

Kahana has changed. There's a large Filipino camp now, and Filipino bachelors make up half of the work force. Tall eucalyptus ring the village, and every yard is an orchard of mango, avocado, banana, and papaya. The barracks have been replaced by detached wood frame houses with asphalt-shingle roofs. The air is bracing.

Aunt Kitano is already dead when we get there, and Sadao and his stepfather are standing face-to-face and shouting.

"That's why I came back, to look after her!" Sadao towers over him.

"I want her buried here so I can visit her!" Mr. Kitano shouts.

"I insist on cremating her!" Sadao shouts back down at him.

"I want her buried!"

"I want to take her with me!"

"I am her husband!"

"I am her son!"

Isao pulls Sadao aside. "Why don't you agree with him for now. After he dies, you can dig up her bones, cremate them, and take them with you."

I help wash and dress the body. I think of Madame Kanai's worrying about "dying in a strange land." You're fortunate, Kitano-san; you have people fighting over you.

"You should rest," Isao says.

"I have to do this last thing for her."

"She was your substitute," Kiyoshi says.

"I'm such a nobody, and twice I've been saved."

25 · Dream of Kahana

The next week I tottered to Dr. Hamaguchi's office on Front Street and got fitted for dentures. It seemed so strange. Nothing had changed in the rest of the world. Nobody knew or cared how sick I'd been. "The disease of poverty is worse than all 404 diseases," the proverb says. It's nonsense. The disease of the body is the worst. Poverty is secondary. What if the dentures added another $100 to our $5,500 debt? All the riches in the world can't make up for a fatal disease.

Sadao-san drove to the house several days later. His face was puffed and his eyes swollen.

"I'm moving out. I can't stand that Kitano wretch," he said.

"Please *gaman*. Your mother would be so pleased," I said, flapping my lips. "She needs forty-nine days of quiet to settle her affairs on earth."

Aunt Kitano had run off to Hawaii soon after her father's death. I didn't want Sadao to repeat her mistake.

Several weeks later I got my dentures. They filled my cheeks and restored my voice and taste buds. The fish and rice were so delicious. I was ravenous. All the worrying about the debt fell away like flaky skin.

Mr. Handa, our landlord, came to the house. "The quarters behind the store are too cramped for the four of us," he said.

I would've been crushed without my teeth, but I enunciated with formality, "Thank you so much for all the extensions. You have been so kind. We will pay you back for certain."

I appreciated his saving our face. A *gaijin* would've evicted us outright.

A few days later another scandal shook Omiya Camp. Kimura Kazuo, a nisei in his twenties, was arrested for robbing the bank in the little town of Haiku, east of Kahului. Why did he do it? Nobody knew. Nobody in Kahana would dream of doing such a thing. He must've hated plantation work; he'd done odd jobs around town. It was fortunate he was caught immediately and was now out of sight in the county jail somewhere. It would've been awful for his parents if he'd been arrested here and led away in handcuffs for all Pepelau to see.

"We should go back to Kahana," I told Isao.

"Shimomura will rent me a house," he said.

"We need to move now."

"The fishing will turn around."

"Let's give it one more year. If it hasn't turned around by then, let's go back. $6,000 is the limit. Anything larger would be too big a burden on the children," I said.

The new house was like a barracks. Three rooms without doors were lined up in a row. Mr. Shimomura dug a cesspool and added a toilet and kitchen. Toshio had one end room all to himself. In the middle was the parlor, then our bedroom. We slept under the same mosquito net, on the same futons—Isao and myself on one end, Joji and Kiyoshi on the other, Takako and Miwa in the middle. We shared the neighbor's bath. *Well,* I thought, *at least we're a block closer to Kahana.*

Sadao Ono, or Anshan as the children called him, endured the forty-nine days with his stepfather, then transferred to the Pepelau Carpenter Shop and moved to the single men's quarters below the mill. He'd never drank during Prohibition, but now he brought a bottle of whiskey and drank with Isao. When Isao was out, he'd talk to Joji and Kiyoshi.

"Oooo, me, *kuro shita.* . . . Ebery time I maku mistaki, he *kotsun* my head. Ooooo, hardo. Ooooo, you mama too *kuro shita.* . . . You grandmama, she *oni,*" he said, using his index fingers as horns.

Hmmm . . . old stories don't die even when I bury them, I thought. Aunt Kitano repeated them to Sadao, and now Sadao told them to Joji and Kiyoshi. They never tired of listening to Sadao's stories, whereas Toshio would walk away, saying, "Yeah, I wen hear that story already."

Sadao reminded me of Mr. Ando, the tinsmith who'd hanged himself. Both had been educated in Japan, and now the Hawaii-grown nisei made fun of their broken English.

"He acts like a know-it-all after a couple of drinks," Isao said.

One night Isao must've craved whiskey. He sat on the folding tatami mat on the parlor floor and drank with Sadao from a water glass. I was at the Singer. I was getting orders now for khaki and blue denim pants at 50 cents a pair. I could cut and sew a pair in a couple of hours.

I heard snippets of their laconic conversation every time I lifted my foot from the motor.

During one such lull Sadao said, ". . . ne, elder brother? You've been a fisherman now for over fourteen years. You should give it nine more months, ne? If you haven't succeeded by then, you should quit, ne?"

It felt uncanny. Aunt Kitano was speaking from the grave.

Isao jumped up and left in a huff.

"I can't see how he can drink and go to work every day. Tell him not to come so often," Isao grumbled later that night.

"We're his family. He's welcome any time. It's my repayment to Aunt Kitano," I said.

They're like children, I thought. But Toshio was the real worry. After Mr. Roosevelt was elected president, they passed a law forbidding minors to work all those hours. But Toshio still spent all his time at the employee's room above Aoki Store.

"Why can't you come home earlier?" I asked.

"I have to study."

"Why can't you study here?"

"How can I? You don't even have a table and chair. It's only good for sleeping."

"What about the kitchen table and bench?"

"It's not the same thing."

❋   ❋   ❋

I was happy Isao found me attractive again, but now I worried about waking up the children. They were bigger now and the space was more cramped. But the bigger worry was getting pregnant.

Then I missed a month and then another. How did the *haole* women manage to have so few babies? We should learn their secret.

I told Isao, "We have to go back now. We'll save $50 if we move back in time. We don't have Aunt Kitano anymore."

"The fishing will turn around," he said.

"You've been saying that for the last six years. We can go to another plantation camp if you feel you'll lose face returning to Kahana. But all our *kosai* is in Kahana."

He started to leave.

"It hurts, but we have to talk about it," I said, surprised that I hadn't raised my voice.

Why was he so stubborn? It's not that he lacked perseverance. His perseverance went in the wrong direction and became stubborn pride. So what if Mr. Kawai and the old steam plow gang laughed at him and called him a failure? They need not know how large our debt is. *That* would be a big loss of face. We could pretend it was the new child. Fishing couldn't support six children. We could say that at least we tried. The others didn't have the courage or the foolhardiness. Which often is the same thing.

* * *

"What's the debt now?" Toshio asked one day.

"About $5,500."

"Papa should quit fishing. Aoki, Tani, and the others should refuse him credit and force him to quit. They don't because they figure his sons will pay up. I bet you they'd have refused him long ago if not for me, Joji, and Kiyo."

"He'll be quitting soon."

"He said so?"

"No."

"How do you know?"

"I know."

"How?"

"I feel it in my guts," I said.

Why didn't I tell him then? I thought afterward, *This new child will give him the excuse to quit.* I felt ridiculous being cowed by my own child.

* * *

Maybe it was because of the new life inside me. I longed for Kahana. I recalled fragments of a haiku from long, long ago: a

150

woman waits—*matsu* 待 —for her lover under a pine tree— *matsu* 松 . Aunt Kitano's funeral had been like a grand reunion. The whole village had turned out. Mrs. Shiotsugu, who used to make us convulse with laughter at the laundry, now had seven sons. The eldest had begun working at age fourteen and was now sending his younger brothers to Pepelau High School. Mrs. Toyama, whose Singer sat next to mine when Mr. Terada taught us smocking, had six. Her older boy and girl went directly into the fields after grade school. The Kahana people all had large families, unlike the townspeople here. A father's plantation pay by itself couldn't support his big family, so the children went to work.

Mrs. Kuni, the widow, still had her candy store and barbershop. She'd skimped and saved and sent her son to the normal school in Honolulu, and now her son Robert and his wife (who had been Kiyoshi's teacher at Liliuokalani) were grade school teachers. Her patience and perseverance had produced success.

"You should come back. So much has changed. It's nicer," Shinagawa Emi-chan said. Ever since her husband had died from an infection in his nostril, she had supported her three children by working in the fields. She'd been so frail. Now she was tanned and robust. She, too, was succeeding without her man.

I missed bathing and talking story with them. The baths were separate now. The scum from the men's bath no longer floated over to the women's side. The pay was now $1 a day for irrigation and 65 cents for weeding. Rent, water, kerosene, and medical care were still free. Everything would be cared for.

One night Toshio came home from Aoki Store and shouted, "Why didn't you tell me you were having a baby?! I'm always the last to know! I'm not having anything more to do with you folks!"

"But you promised to help!"

"With the debt! Not with raising your and Papa's children!" He stormed out.

I should have told him, I thought. *I'll be showing in a couple of months anyway. But it's so hard talking to him.* I'd sent Joji earlier in the day to Aoki Store. They had a sale on diapers. The women clerks at the store must've teased Toshio.

Toshio spent the night at the employees' room at Aoki Store. I made corned beef patties in the morning for his lunch, but he didn't show up. Did he go to Pepelau High in yesterday's clothes? Where did he bathe? What did he do for lunch?

When Isao came home from sea, I waited till he sat down at the kitchen table with his beer. Then I told him about Toshio.

"He's a crybaby," he scoffed.

"He has every right to complain. We're going to lose him if we keep on like this."

He sighed, "I feel like I'm being squeezed to death."

"It's the children who are being squeezed."

"You must be tired." The three sentences were my ritual greeting—welcome home; you must be tired; how was it? I could tell how bad the catch was by how badly his shoulders sagged. Today he looked crushed. "How was it?" I hated asking.

He let out a deep sigh and said under his breath, "I'll have to sell the boat first."

We'll save $50 if we move before August! I almost blurted.

He ran his hand down his face. "I have to talk to Tani. I owe him. I'm his only source."

"We've got our health. That's the important thing."

"Then I feel bad about Shimomura. He'd fixed this place just for us."

"We're a success compared to many families. We've escaped premature deaths."

"What?" He looked up.

"It was nothing." I got up quietly and went back to the Singer in the parlor. I'd left an unfinished pair of denim pants on it. It was the fourth pair of the day, earning us $2. The machine was such a comfort—it not only brought in money but also its noise drowned out my worries. I'd stoop over it for hours, forgetting time.

But as soon as I sat down, my heart fluttered and my thoughts raced. *How am I going to tell Toshio he'll have to quit school and go to work in the fields? He'll have had at least two years of Pepelau High. Joji won't even see the inside of a high school. Neither will Kiyoshi when he finishes at Kahana Grade School. They'll have lots of company in Kahana. It'd be nice if we could move before the new school year at the latest. It'd be a new beginning for everyone . . .*

Glossary

A (H) indicates a Hawaiian word. All other words are Japanese.

aburage   deep fried tofu used for cone sushi

aji   horse mackerel

Akemashite omedetoh   a greeting on the first three days of the New
   Year (lit., happy dawning)

amaeru   to act up, begging to be pampered; it reinforces dependence

Amaterasu Omikami   sun goddess of Japanese mythology

anshan   contraction of ani-san or elder brother

baka   fool

bakatare   damn fool

Benkei   a big heroic warrior-priest of the twelfth century

chikusho!   beast!

fugu   Pacific puffer

gaijin   non-Japanese (lit., outsider)

go-chiso sama   It was most delicious (said after a meal)

hakama   men's formal divided skirt

hana (H)   work

haole (H)   white person (lit., foreigner)

haori   a short coat

hapa (H)   person of mixed blood

hi-ake   thirtieth or thirty-third day after birth when the child is
   taken for his or her first visit to the Shinto shrine (lit., dawn)

hidoi   harsh

hila hila (H)   shame

iriko   small minnow-like fish that has been dried and salted

issei   first generation immigrant

itai   it hurts

kage Benkei   phantom Benkei (see Benkei)

kakure   underground Christian during the persecution

Kami-sama   Christian God

Kanaka   a native Hawaiian

kapakahi (H)   biased; upside down

karuta   a children's card game, using the Japanese alphabet and sayings

kibei   nisei who studied in Japan (lit., returnee to America)

kiawe (H)   algaroba tree

kokua (H)   help

kokua shite   help me (see *shite*)

kolohe (H)   rascal

komban wa   Good evening

kompan   group sharing work on designated field

kosai   network of mutual obligations (lit., contact, social exchange)

kotsun   sound of a rap to the head

kozo   apprentice

kuro shita   I suffered

Kyokai   Christian church

lolo (H)   dumb

luna (H)   foreman

mahimahi (H)   dolphin fish

makai (H)   toward the sea

miso   soybean paste

mochi   pounded rice dumpling

Nasu-no-Yoichi   famous archer of the twelfth century

nigari   bittern

nishime   a country stew of chicken, radish, carrots, shiitake mushooms, aburage, bamboo shoots, kelp, and taro roots

obaban   granny (Aunt Kitano)

ohai (H)   monkeypod tree

okusama   Madame (lit., Madame Interior; wife of feudal lord)

oni   devil

ozoni   broth containing *mochi*

paka (H)   red snapper (short for *opakapaka*)

pali (H)   cliff

pau (H)   finished

piitare   stingy

San-O-sama   Shinto deity, guardian of Ikeura Village

shashin   photograph

shiran   I don't know

shite   imperative mode of *suru* (to do)

soba   buckwheat noodle

sumimasen   I am sorry

tabi   sock made from woven cloth with split at the big toe for wear
   with zori

tada ima!   I'm home! (lit., now!)

tanomimasu   I beseech you

tanomoshi   a mutual financing group

uchi Benkei   a Benkei when at home (see Benkei)

uchi ni kaereba tenka sama   a world ruler whenever he returns
   home

Urashima Taro   a Rip van Winkle of Japanese fairy tale

yakamashii   Shut up (lit., noisy)

About the Author

MILTON ATSUSHI MURAYAMA was born in Lahaina, Maui, and grew up in Lahaina and Puukolii, a sugar plantation company town that no longer exists. He attended Lahainaluna High School. During World War II he trained at the Military Intelligence Language School at Camp Savage, Minnesota, and served as an interpreter in India and China. Murayama received a BA in English from the University of Hawaii and an MA in Chinese and Japanese from Columbia University. He has worked at various jobs and has lived in Minneapolis, New York, and Washington, D.C. He presently resides in San Francisco with his wife. Murayama is the author of *All I Asking for Is My Body* and has written a play based on it. *Five Years on a Rock* and *All I Asking* form the first two parts of a tetralogy.